William Shakespeare

The Comedy of E

In Plain and Simple Eng.

BookCaps Study Guides
www.bookcaps.com

Table of Contents

About This Series

The "Classic Retold" series started as a way of telling classics for the modern reader—being careful to preserve the themes and integrity of the original. Whether you want to understand Shakespeare a little more or are trying to get a better grasps of the Greek classics, there is a book waiting for you!

The series is expanding every month. Visit BookCaps.com to see all the books in the series, and while you are there join the Facebook page, so you are first to know when a new book comes out.

Characters

SOLINUS, Duke of Ephesus.

AEGEON, a Merchant of Syracuse.

ANTIPHOLUS OF EPHESUS, Twin brothers and sons to Aegion and ANTIPHOLUS OF SYRACUSE, and Aemelia, but unknown to each other.

DROMIO OF EPHESUS, Twin brothers, and attendants on DROMIO OF SYRACUSE, the two Antipholuses.

BALTHAZAR, a Merchant.

ANGELO, a Goldsmith.

A MERCHANT, friend to Antipholus of Syracuse.

PINCH, a Schoolmaster and a Conjurer.

AEMILIA, Wife to Aegeon, an Abbess at Ephesus

ADRIANA, Wife to Antipholus of Ephesus

LUCIANA, her Sister. LUCE, her Servant.

Play

Act 1

SCENE I. A hall in DUKE SOLINUS'S palace.

Enter DUKE SOLINUS, AEGEON, Gaoler, Officers, and other Attendants

AEGEON
Proceed, Solinus, to procure my fall
And by the doom of death end woes and all.

Go ahead, Solinus, secure my downfall
Doom me to die and end all of my misery.

DUKE SOLINUS
Merchant of Syracuse, plead no more;
I am not partial to infringe our laws:
The enmity and discord which of late
Sprung from the rancorous outrage of your duke
To merchants, our well-dealing countrymen,
Who wanting guilders to redeem their lives
Have seal'd his rigorous statutes with their bloods,
Excludes all pity from our threatening looks.
For, since the mortal and intestine jars
'Twixt thy seditious countrymen and us,
It hath in solemn synods been decreed
Both by the Syracusians and ourselves,
To admit no traffic to our adverse towns   Nay, more,
If any born at Ephesus be seen
At any Syracusian marts and fairs;
Again: if any Syracusian born
Come to the bay of Ephesus, he dies,
His goods confiscate to the duke's dispose,
Unless a thousand marks be levied,
To quit the penalty and to ransom him.
Thy substance, valued at the highest rate,
Cannot amount unto a hundred marks;
Therefore by law thou art condemned to die.

Merchant of Syracuse, stop pleading with me;
I am not the type to bend our laws:
The hatred and disagreement which recently
Came from the bitter outrage of your duke
To merchants, our well-dealing countrymen,
Who wanting money to redeem their lives
Have paid their blood for this harsh   laws,
Leaves no room for pity in our threatening looks.
Since the violent and deadly conflicts started
Between your rebellious countrymen and us,
In solemn councils of church it has been decreed
Both by the Syracusians and ourselves,
That no one from either town will be allowed in the other. No, more than that,
If anyone born in Ephesus is seen
At any Syracusian marts and fairs;
Likewise: if anyone who is Syracusian born
Comes to the bay of Ephesus, he dies,
His goods confiscated for the duke's disposal,
Unless someone can pay a thousand marks,
To stop the penalty and ransom him.
Your goods, valued at the highest rate,
Cannot amount to even a hundred marks;
Therefore by law you are condemned to die.

AEGEON
Yet this my comfort: when your words are done,
My woes end likewise with the evening sun.

At least I have this: when your words are done,
My misery will end with the evening sun.

DUKE SOLINUS
Well, Syracusian, say in brief the cause
Why thou departed'st from thy native home
And for what cause thou camest to Ephesus.

Well, Syracusian, briefly explain the cause of
Why you left your native home
And why you came to Ephesus.

AEGEON

A heavier task could not have been imposed
Than I to speak my griefs unspeakable:
Yet, that the world may witness that my end
Was wrought by nature, not by vile offence,
I'll utter what my sorrows give me leave.
In Syracusa was I born, and wed

You couldn't have imposed a heavier task
Than to make me speak my unspeakable griefs:
Yet, so the world can witness that my death
Was brought about without meaning to offend,
I'll utter what I can about my sorrows.
In Syracusa was I born, and married
Unto a woman, happy but for me,
And by me, had not our hap been bad.
With her I lived in joy; our wealth increased   By prosperous voyages I often made
To Epidamnum; till my factor's death
And the great care of goods at random left
Drew me from kind embracements of my spouse:
From whom my absence was not six months old
Before herself, almost at fainting under
The pleasing punishment that women bear,
Had made provision for her following me
And soon and safe arrived where I was.
There had she not been long, but she became
A joyful mother of two goodly sons;
And, which was strange, the one so like the other,
As could not be distinguish'd but by names.
That very hour, and in the self-same inn,
A meaner woman was delivered
Of such a burden, male twins, both alike:
Those,--for their parents were exceeding poor,--
I bought and brought up to attend my sons.
My wife, not meanly proud of two such boys,
Made daily motions for our home return:
Unwilling I agreed. Alas! too soon,
We came aboard.
A league from Epidamnum had we sail'd,
Before the always wind-obeying deep
Gave any tragic instance of our harm:
But longer did we not retain much hope;
For what obscured light the heavens did grant
Did but convey unto our fearful minds
A doubtful warrant of immediate death;
Which though myself would gladly have embraced,
Yet the incessant weepings of my wife,
Weeping before for what she saw must come,
And piteous plainings of the pretty babes,
That mourn'd for fashion, ignorant what to fear,
Forced me to seek delays for them and me.
And this it was, for other means was none:

The sailors sought for safety by our boat,
And left the ship, then sinking-ripe, to us:
My wife, more careful for the latter-born,
Had fasten'd him unto a small spare mast,
Such as seafaring men provide for storms;
To him one of the other twins was bound,
Whilst I had been like heedful of the other:
The children thus disposed, my wife and I,
Fixing our eyes on whom our care was fix'd,
Fasten'd ourselves at either end the mast;
And floating straight, obedient to the stream,
Was carried towards Corinth, as we thought.

To a woman, who was happy until she met me,
I could've made her happy, had luck been better.
With her I lived in joy; our wealth increased   By prosperous voyages I often made
To Epidamnum; till my agent's death
And the burden of caring for the rest of my goods
Took me away from my wife's embrace:
I was not gone six months
Before she, about to faint under
The pain of pregnancy,
Had made arrangements to follow me
And soon and safe arrived where I was.
Not long afterwards she became
A joyful mother of two twin sons;
It was strange, each one so like the other,
That the only thing telling them apart was their names.
That very hour, and in the self-same inn,
A lower-class woman delivered
Similarly, male twins, both alike:
Those,--for their parents were exceedingly poor,-
I bought and raised to serve my sons.
My wife, extremely proud of two such boys,
Begged me daily for our home return:
Unwilling, I agreed. Unfortunately, we came aboard too soon.
We had sailed a league from Epidamnum,
Before the sea that always obeys the wind
Gave any signs of danger:
Before too long we had no hope left;
The mass covering the light from the heavens
Made us, in our fear-stricken state
Believe that we were facing immediate death;
Which I myself would have gladly   embraced,
But my wife's ceaseless sobbing,
Weeping for what she saw about to happen,
And pitiful cries of our beautiful babies,
Crying without even understanding what to fear,
Forced me to seek a way for us to survive.
This is what I did, since I had no other choice:
The sailors had all abandoned ship,
Taking the safety boats and leaving us to sink:
My wife, more concerned for the younger son,
Had tied him onto a small spare mast,
Such as seafaring men provide for storms;
She then tied one of the other twins to him,
While I did the same to the remaining two:

With the children taken care of, my wife and I,
Locking eyes,
Fastened ourselves to either end of the mast;
And floating straight, obedient to the current,
Were carried towards Corinth, or so we thought.
At length the sun, gazing upon the earth,
Dispersed those vapours that offended us;
And by the benefit of his wished light,
The seas wax'd calm, and we discovered   Two ships from far making amain to us,
Of Corinth that, of Epidaurus this:
But ere they came,--O, let me say no more!
Gather the sequel by that went before.

After a while the sun, gazing upon the earth
Dispersed those terrible clouds;
And because of his much wished-for light,
The seas became calm, and we discovered   Two far-off ships coming towards us,
One from Corinth the other from Epidaurus:
But before they came,-- O, I can't say any more!
You can guess what happened by what I've said.

DUKE SOLINUS
Nay, forward, old man; do not break off so;
For we may pity, though not pardon thee.

No, keep going, old man; don't leave it like that;
We may take pity, though we won't pardon you.

AEGEON

O, had the gods done so, I had not now
Worthily term'd them merciless to us!
For, ere the ships could meet by twice five leagues,
We were encounterd by a mighty rock;
Which being violently borne upon,
Our helpful ship was splitted in the midst;
So that, in this unjust divorce of us,
Fortune had left to both of us alike
What to delight in, what to sorrow for.
Her part, poor soul! seeming as burdened
With lesser weight but not with lesser woe,
Was carried with more speed before the wind;
And in our sight they three were taken up
By fishermen of Corinth, as we thought.
At length, another ship had seized on us;
And, knowing whom it was their hap to save,
Gave healthful welcome to their shipwreck'd guests;
And would have reft the fishers of their prey,
Had not their bark been very slow of sail;
And therefore homeward did they bend their course.
Thus have you heard me sever'd from my bliss;
That by misfortunes was my life prolong'd,
To tell sad stories of my own mishaps.

O, if only the gods had taken pity, I would
Not now be rightfully calling them merciless!
Because before the ships reached within ten leagues of us,
We were met by a huge rock;
And since we were moving so fast,
It split our ship down the middle;
So that, as we were unjustly separated,
Fortune had left to each of us
Something to delight in as well as to sorrow for.
For her, poor soul! Since she was burdened
With less weight, but not with less misfortune,
Was carried away with more speed by the wind;
And I saw her and the babies taken up
By fishermen of Corinth, or so I thought.
At length, another ship had reached us;
And, knowing who they were lucky to be saving,
Were welcoming and took good care of us, their shipwrecked guests;
And would have gone to rescue my wife,
If their ship hadn't been so slow to sail;
And so they changed course to sail towards home.
Now you see how I was severed from my bliss;
That because of bad luck my life was prolonged,
To tell sad stories of my own mishaps.

DUKE SOLINUS
And for the sake of them thou sorrowest for,
Do me the favour to dilate at full
What hath befall'n of them and thee till now.

And for the sake of those you lost,
Do me the favor to expand your tale, and tell me
What became of them and you up until now.

AEGEON
My youngest boy, and yet my eldest care,
At eighteen years became inquisitive
After his brother: and importuned me
That his attendant--so his case was like,
Reft of his brother, but retain'd his name--
Might bear him company in the quest of him,
Whom whilst I labour'd of a love to see,
I hazarded the loss of whom I loved.

My youngest boy, the one I care for the most,
At eighteen years old started to wonder
About his brother: and begged me
To let his attendant—who also
Lost his brother, but at least knew his name--
Go with him in search of their twins,
And since I also wanted to see my lost son,
I risked losing the one I loved to find the other.
Five summers have I spent in furthest Greece,
Roaming clean through the bounds of Asia,
And, coasting homeward, came to Ephesus; Hopeless to find, yet loath to leave unsought
Or that or any place that harbours men.
But here must end the story of my life;
And happy were I in my timely death,
Could all my travels warrant me they live.

I spent five years in the furthest parts of Greece,
Roaming throughout all of Asia,
And, making my way home, came to Ephesus;   with no hope of finding, yet unwilling to stop,
I will search any place where men live.
But here must end the story of my life;
And I would be happy that my time has come,
If all my travels could prove to me that they live.

DUKE SOLINUS
Hapless Aegeon, whom the fates have mark'd
To bear the extremity of dire mishap!
Now, trust me, were it not against our laws,
Against my crown, my oath, my dignity,
Which princes, would they, may not   disannul,
My soul would sue as advocate for thee.
But, though thou art adjudged to the death
And passed sentence may not be recall'd
But to our honour's great disparagement,
Yet I will favour thee in what I can.
Therefore, merchant, I'll limit thee this day
To seek thy life by beneficial help:
Try all the friends thou hast in Ephesus;
Beg thou, or borrow, to make up the sum,
And live; if no, then thou art doom'd to die.
Gaoler, take him to thy custody.

Poor Aegeon, the fates have marked you
To suffer the extremities of terrible misfortune!
Now, trust me, if it wasn't against our laws,
Against my crown, my oath, my dignity,
Which even princes, if they wanted, could not disobey
My own soul would support your case.
But, though you have been sentenced to death,
And passed sentence cannot be taken back
Without greatly discrediting my honor,
I will help you in any way I can.
Therefore, merchant, I will give you one day
To seek help to save your life:
Try all the friends you have in Ephesus;
Beg, borrow, do what you can to make ransom,
And live; if you can't, you are doomed to die.
Jailor, take him to your custody.

Jailor
I will, my lord.

I will, my lord.

AEGEON
Hopeless and helpless doth AEgeon wend,
But to procrastinate his lifeless end.

I will go, hopeless and helpless,
Only putting off my death.

Exeunt

SCENE II. The Mart.

Enter ANTIPHOLUS of Syracuse, DROMIO of Syracuse, and FIRST MERCHANT

FIRST MERCHANT
Therefore give out you are of Epidamnum,
Lest that your goods too soon be confiscate.
This very day a Syracusian merchant
Is apprehended for arrival here;
And not being able to buy out his life
According to the statute of the town,
Dies ere the weary sun set in the west.
There is your money that I had to keep.

So tell people you are from Epidamnum,
Otherwise they will confiscate your goods.
Just today a Syracusian merchant
Was apprehended for arriving here;
And since he could not pay ransom
According to the law of the town,
He is going to die before sunset.
There is your money that I had to keep.

ANTIPHOLUS OF SYRACUSE
Go bear it to the Centaur, where we host,
And stay there, Dromio, till I come to thee.
Within this hour it will be dinner-time:
Till that, I'll view the manners of the town,
Peruse the traders, gaze upon the buildings,
And then return and sleep within mine inn,
For with long travel I am stiff and weary.
Get thee away.

Go take it to the Centaur, where we are staying
And stay there, Dromio, till I come find you.
It will be dinner-time within the hour:
Till then I'm going to get to know the town,
Peruse the traders, gaze upon the buildings,
And then return and sleep at the inn,
Since I am stiff and weary from traveling.
Go on, get going.

DROMIO OF SYRACUSE
Many a man would take you at your word,
And go indeed, having so good a mean.

Many men would take that literally,
And run off with all the money you just gave me.

Exit

ANTIPHOLUS OF SYRACUSE
A trusty villain, sir, that very oft,
When I am dull with care and melancholy,
Lightens my humour with his merry jests.
What, will you walk with me about the town,
And then go to my inn and dine with me?

What a trustworthy rascal he is, that so often,
When I am feeling down, worried or melancholy,
Lightens my mood with his merry jokes.
Well, will you walk with me about the town,
And then go to my inn and dine with me?

FIRST MERCHANT
I am invited, sir, to certain merchants,
Of whom I hope to make much benefit;
I crave your pardon. Soon at five o'clock,
Please you, I'll meet with you upon the mart
And afterward consort you till bed-time:
My present business calls me from you now.

I have been invited, sir, to see certain merchants,
Whom I hope to make good money from;
I beg your pardon. Soon at five o'clock,
If it please you, I'll meet with you at the market
And we can talk until you decide to go to bed:
My present business calls me from you now.

ANTIPHOLUS OF SYRACUSE
Farewell till then: I will go lose myself
And wander up and down to view the city.

Farewell till then: I will go lose myself
And wander up and down to view the city.

FIRST MERCHANT
Sir, I commend you to your own content.

Sir, I hope you will be contented.

Exit

ANTIPHOLUS OF SYRACUSE
He that commends me to mine own content
Commends me to the thing I cannot get.
I to the world am like a drop of water
That in the ocean seeks another drop,
Who, falling there to find his fellow forth,
Unseen, inquisitive, confounds himself:
So I, to find a mother and a brother,
In quest of them, unhappy, lose myself.

He that hopes that I will be contented
Hopes me to be something I cannot.
To the world, I am like a drop of water
In the ocean looking for another drop,
Who, falling in to find it,
Unseen, inquisitive, confuses himself:
So I, looking for a mother and a brother,
Searching for them, unhappy, lose myself.

Enter DROMIO of Ephesus

Here comes the almanac of my true date.
What now? how chance thou art return'd so soon?

Here comes the one that shares my birth date.
What now? How is it that you've returned so soon?

DROMIO OF EPHESUS
Return'd so soon! rather approach'd too late:
The capon burns, the pig falls from the spit,
The clock hath strucken twelve upon the bell;
My mistress made it one upon my cheek:
She is so hot because the meat is cold;
The meat is cold because you come not home;
You come not home because you have no stomach;
You have no stomach having broke your fast;
But we that know what 'tis to fast and   pray
Are penitent for your default to-day.

Returned so soon! More like approached too late:
The food is burnt, the pig fell off the spit,
The clock has struck the bell twelve times;
And my mistress struck me one on my cheek:
She's all fired up hot because the meat is cold;
The meat is cold because you've not been home;
You've not been home because you aren't hungry;
You're not hungry because you ate breakfast;
But poor people like me who know what it's like to fast and pray
Are being punished for your faults today.

ANTIPHOLUS OF SYRACUSE
Stop in your wind, sir: tell me this, I pray:
Where have you left the money that I gave you?

Stop right there: tell me, please:
Where have you left the money that I gave you?

DROMIO OF EPHESUS
O,--sixpence, that I had o' Wednesday last
To pay the saddler for my mistress' crupper?
The saddler had it, sir; I kept it not.

O,-- the sixpence, that I had on last Wednesday
To pay the saddler for my mistress' riding gear?
The saddler has it, sir; I didn't keep it.

ANTIPHOLUS OF SYRACUSE
I am not in a sportive humour now:
Tell me, and dally not, where is the money?
We being strangers here, how darest thou trust
So great a charge from thine own custody?

I am not in the mood for jokes now:
Tell me, and quit goofing, where is the money?
We're strangers here, how could you dare let
So much money out of your sight?

DROMIO OF EPHESUS
I pray you, sir, as you sit at dinner:
I from my mistress come to you in post;
If I return, I shall be post indeed,
For she will score your fault upon my pate.
Methinks your maw, like mine, should be your clock,
And strike you home without a messenger.

I beg you, sir, joke as you sit at dinner:
I come to you from my mistress in a hurry;
If I return without you, she'll beat me good,
And take her anger at you out on me.
I would think your hunger, like mine, would be your clock, and make you strike for home without
needing a messenger.

ANTIPHOLUS OF SYRACUSE
Come, Dromio, come, these jests are out of season;
Reserve them till a merrier hour than this.
Where is the gold I gave in charge to thee?
Oh come on, Dromio, these jokes are getting out of hand;
Tell them at a happier time than this.
Where is the gold I left you in charge of?

DROMIO OF EPHESUS
To me, sir? why, you gave no gold to me.

To me, sir? why, you gave no gold to me.

ANTIPHOLUS OF SYRACUSE
Come on, sir knave, have done your foolishness,
And tell me how thou hast disposed thy charge.

Come on, sir idiot, quit fooling around,
Tell me how you've disposed of your charge.

DROMIO OF EPHESUS
My charge was but to fetch you from the mart
Home to your house, the Phoenix, sir, to dinner:
My mistress and her sister stays for you.
My charge was only to fetch you from the mart
Home to your house, the Phoenix, sir, to dinner:
My mistress and her sister are waiting for you.

ANTIPHOLUS OF SYRACUSE
In what safe place you have bestow'd my money,
Or I shall break that merry sconce of yours
That stands on tricks when I am undisposed:
Where is the thousand marks thou hadst of me?

Tell me what safe place you've left my money,
Or I am going to break that merry head of yours
That keep cracking jokes when I'm in no mood:
Where is the thousand marks you got from me?

DROMIO OF EPHESUS
I have some marks of yours upon my pate,
Some of my mistress' marks upon my shoulders,
But not a thousand marks between you both.
If I should pay your worship those again,
Perchance you will not bear them patiently.

I have some marks of yours upon my head,
Some of my mistress' marks upon my shoulders,
But not a thousand marks between you both.
If I were to give you those marks back you probably wouldn't like it.

ANTIPHOLUS OF SYRACUSE
Thy mistress' marks? what mistress, slave, hast thou?

Your mistress' marks? what mistress are you talking about, slave?

DROMIO OF EPHESUS
Your worship's wife, my mistress at the Phoenix;
She that doth fast till you come home to dinner,
And prays that you will hie you home to dinner.

Your wife, my mistress, at the Phoenix;
She who doesn't eat until you come home,
And prays that you will hurry home to dinner.

ANTIPHOLUS OF SYRACUSE
What, wilt thou flout me thus unto my face,
Being forbid? There, take you that, sir knave.

What, are you making fun of me to my face,
When I told you to stop? There, take that, stupid.

DROMIO OF EPHESUS
What mean you, sir? for God's sake, hold your hands!
Nay, and you will not, sir, I'll take my heels.

What do you mean, sir? for God's sake, stop hitting me!
No, you're not stopping, sir, so I'll run away

Exit

ANTIPHOLUS OF SYRACUSE
Upon my life, by some device or other
The villain is o'er-raught of all my money.
They say this town is full of cozenage,
As, nimble jugglers that deceive the eye,
Dark-working sorcerers that change the mind,
Soul-killing witches that deform the body,
Disguised cheaters, prating mountebanks,
And many such-like liberties of sin:
If it prove so, I will be gone the sooner.
I'll to the Centaur, to go seek this slave:
I greatly fear my money is not safe.

I can't believe it, somehow that   Rascal has cheated me out of all my money.
They say this town is full of tricks and deception,
Like nimble jugglers that deceive the eye,
Dark-working sorcerers that change the mind,
Soul-killing witches that deform the body,
Disguised cheaters, fast-talking swindlers,
And many other such sinful activities:
If that's the case I'd like to leave all the sooner.
I'll to the Centaur, to go find that slave of mine:
I greatly fear my money is not safe.

Exit

Act 2

SCENE I. The house of ANTIPHOLUS of Ephesus.

Enter ADRIANA and LUCIANA

ADRIANA
Neither my husband nor the slave return'd,
That in such haste I sent to seek his master!
Sure, Luciana, it is two o'clock.

Neither my husband has returned nor the slave,
I sent off to quickly seek his master!
Luciana, it is already two o'clock.

LUCIANA
Perhaps some merchant hath invited him,
And from the mart he's somewhere gone to dinner.
Good sister, let us dine and never fret:
A man is master of his liberty:
Time is their master, and, when they see time,
They'll go or come: if so, be patient, sister.

Perhaps another merchant has invited him,
And he left the mart to go somewhere else for dinner.
Good sister, we should stop worrying and eat:
A man is master of his freedom:
And time is master of them, when they see the time, they will come or go: be patient, sister.

ADRIANA
Why should their liberty than ours be more?

Why should they have more freedom than us?

LUCIANA
Because their business still lies out o' door.

Because their business is out of the home.

ADRIANA
Look, when I serve him so, he takes it ill.

Look, he doesn't like it when I'm like this.

LUCIANA
O, know he is the bridle of your will.

O, he is the bridle of your will.

ADRIANA
There's none but asses will be bridled so.

Only a mule would want to be bridled like that.

LUCIANA
Why, headstrong liberty is lash'd with woe.
There's nothing situate under heaven's eye
But hath his bound, in earth, in sea, in sky:
The beasts, the fishes, and the winged fowls,
Are their males' subjects and at their controls:
Men, more divine, the masters of all these,
Lords of the wide world and wild watery seas,
Indued with intellectual sense and souls,
Of more preeminence than fish and fowls,
Are masters to their females, and their lords:
Then let your will attend on their accords.

Why, headstrong freedom is full of misery.
There's nothing placed under heaven's eye
That isn't bound, in earth, in sea, in sky:
The beasts, the fishes, and the winged birds,
Are all subjects to males and under their control:
Men are more god-like, they master all animals,
Lords of the wide world and wild watery seas,
Endowed with intellectual sense and souls,
Superior to that of fish and birds,
Are masters and lords over their females:
You should do as they wish.

ADRIANA
This servitude makes you to keep unwed.

This servile attitude is keeping you unmarried.

LUCIANA
Not this, but troubles of the marriage-bed.

No, it's not that, it's marriage-bed troubles.

ADRIANA
But, were you wedded, you would bear some sway.

But, if you were married you would have some influence.

LUCIANA
Ere I learn love, I'll practise to obey.

Before I learn to love, I'll learn obedience.

ADRIANA
How if your husband start some other where?

What if your husband goes astray?

LUCIANA
Till he come home again, I would forbear.

I would bear it until he came home again.

ADRIANA
Patience unmoved! no marvel though she pause;
They can be meek that have no other cause.
A wretched soul, bruised with adversity,
We bid be quiet when we hear it cry;
But were we burdened with like weight of pain,
As much or more would we ourselves complain:
So thou, that hast no unkind mate to grieve thee,
With urging helpless patience wouldst relieve me,
But, if thou live to see like right bereft,
This fool-begg'd patience in thee will be left.

That's patience! no wonder she's waiting;
People can be meek if there's no reason not to.
A wretched soul, bruised by hardship,
We tell it to be quiet when we hear it cry;
But if we were burdened by the same pain,
We ourselves would complain as much or more:
So you, with no cruel husband to pain you,
Would try to relive me by urging me to have helpless patience,
But, if you live to see your rights taken away,
This foolish patience in you will be gone.

LUCIANA
Well, I will marry one day, but to try.
Here comes your man; now is your husband nigh.

Well, I will marry one day, just to try it.
Here comes your servant; your husband should follow soon.

Enter DROMIO of Ephesus

ADRIANA
Say, is your tardy master now at hand?

Hey, is your tardy master close at hand?

DROMIO OF EPHESUS
Nay, he's at two hands with me, and that my two ears can witness.

No, he's at two hands with me, as my two ears can attest.

ADRIANA
Say, didst thou speak with him? know'st thou his mind?

Well, did you speak to him? do you know his plan?

DROMIO OF EPHESUS
Ay, ay, he told his mind upon mine ear:
Beshrew his hand, I scarce could understand it.

Yes, yes, he told his plan to my ear:
But no thanks to his hand, I could barely understand it.

LUCIANA
Spake he so doubtfully, thou couldst not feel his meaning?

Did he speak so vaguely, that you couldn't perceive his meaning?

DROMIO OF EPHESUS
Nay, he struck so plainly, I could too well feel his blows; and withal so doubtfully that I could scarce understand them.

No, he hit it so plainly, I could feel his blows all too well; and they were all so bad that I could barely stand under them.

ADRIANA
But say, I prithee, is he coming home? It seems he hath great care to please his wife.

But please, tell me, is he coming home? It seems he's done a great deal to please his wife.

DROMIO OF EPHESUS
Why, mistress, sure my master is horn-mad.

Mistress, my master is like a bull horn-mad.

ADRIANA
Horn-mad, thou villain!

Horn-mad, you jerk!

DROMIO OF EPHESUS
I mean not cuckold-mad;
But, sure, he is stark mad.
When I desired him to come home to dinner,
He ask'd me for a thousand marks in gold:
"Tis dinner-time,' quoth I; 'My gold!' quoth he;
'Your meat doth burn,' quoth I; 'My gold!' quoth he:
'Will you come home?' quoth I; 'My gold!' quoth he.
'Where is the thousand marks I gave thee, villain?'
'The pig,' quoth I, 'is burn'd;' 'My gold!' quoth he:
'My mistress, sir' quoth I; 'Hang up thy mistress!
I know not thy mistress; out on thy   mistress!'

I don't mean that he's a cuckold;
But he is very mad.
When I desired him to come home to dinner,
He asked me for a thousand marks in gold:
"Tis dinner-time,' I said; 'My gold!' he said;
'Your meat is burning,' I said; 'My gold!' he said:
'Will you come home?' I said; 'My gold!' he said.
'Where is the thousand marks I gave you,   idiot?'
'The pig,' I said, 'is burnt;' 'My gold!' he said:
'My mistress, sir' I said; 'Damn your mistress!
I don't know your mistress; who cares about your mistress!'

LUCIANA
Quoth who?

LUCIANA
Who said that?

DROMIO OF EPHESUS
Quoth my master:
'I know,' quoth he, 'no house, no wife, no mistress.'
So that my errand, due unto my tongue,
I thank him, I bare home upon my shoulders;
For, in conclusion, he did beat me there.

My master said that:
'I know,' he said, 'no house, no wife, no   mistress.'
So that my errand, delivered by my tongue,
Thanks to him, I bring home upon my shoulders;
For, at the end of it, that's where he beat me.

ADRIANA
Go back again, thou slave, and fetch him home.

Go back again, you slave, and fetch him home.

DROMIO OF EPHESUS
Go back again, and be new beaten home?
For God's sake, send some other messenger.

Go back again, and be beaten home again?
For God's sake, send some other messenger.

ADRIANA
Back, slave, or I will break thy pate across.

Back, slave, or I will hit you across your face.

DROMIO OF EPHESUS
And he will bless that cross with other beating:
Between you I shall have a holy head.

And he will bless that cross with another beating:
Between the two of you I shall have a holy head.

ADRIANA
Hence, prating peasant! fetch thy master home.

Get out, babbling peasant! get your master home.

DROMIO OF EPHESUS
Am I so round with you as you with me,
That like a football you do spurn me thus?
You spurn me hence, and he will spurn me hither:
If I last in this service, you must case me in leather.

Am I so round with you as you are with me,
That you'll just kick me out like a football?
You kick me here, and he will kick me   there:
If I survive this service, you must cover me in leather.

Exit

LUCIANA
Fie, how impatience loureth in your face!

For shame, your face is covered in impatience!

ADRIANA
His company must do his minions grace,
Whilst I at home starve for a merry look.
Hath homely age the alluring beauty took
From my poor cheek? then he hath wasted it:
Are my discourses dull? barren my wit?
If voluble and sharp discourse be marr'd,
Unkindness blunts it more than marble hard:
Do their gay vestments his affections bait?
That's not my fault: he's master of my state:
What ruins are in me that can be found,
By him not ruin'd? then is he the ground
Of my defeatures. My decayed fair
A sunny look of his would soon repair
But, too unruly deer, he breaks the pale
And feeds from home; poor I am but his stale.

He graces his minions with his presence,
While I'm at home starving for a cheerful look.
Has homely age taken all alluring beauty
From my poor face? it was wasted on him:
Am I boring to talk to? lost my charm?
If my sharp and witty conversation has dulled,
His unkindness blunted like hard marble:
Do their lively clothes win his affections?
That's not my fault: he's master of my clothes:
What can you find about me that is ruined,
That was not ruined by him? he is the reason
For my defects. But my fallen beauty
Would be repaired by one sunny look from him
But, like an unruly deer he breaks the pail
And feeds away from home; I'm only his tool.

LUCIANA
Self-harming jealousy! fie, beat it hence!

Self-harming jealousy! Quit talking like that!

ADRIANA
Unfeeling fools can with such wrongs dispense.
I know his eye doth homage otherwhere,
Or else what lets it but he would be here?
Sister, you know he promised me a chain;
Would that alone, alone he would detain,
So he would keep fair quarter with his bed!
I see the jewel best enamelled
Will lose his beauty; yet the gold bides still,
That others touch, and often touching will
Wear gold: and no man that hath a name,
By falsehood and corruption doth it shame.
Since that my beauty cannot please his eye,
I'll weep what's left away, and weeping die.

Unfeeling fools can ignore such wrongs.
I know his eye is wandering to someone else,
Or why wouldn't he be here?
Sister, you know he promised me a chain;
But I would do without it, if only he would
Remain faithful to his wife!
Even the most beautiful jewel
Will lose its beauty; yet gold lasts forever,
Though if it is touched too often it will
Wear it down: and no man that has a name,
Would dare shame it with lies and corruption.
Since my beauty can no longer please his eye,
I'll weep what's left of it away, and die weeping.

LUCIANA
How many fond fools serve mad jealousy!

How many fools in love entertain such insane jealousy!

Exeunt

SCENE II. A public place.

Enter ANTIPHOLUS of Syracuse

ANTIPHOLUS OF SYRACUSE
The gold I gave to Dromio is laid up
Safe at the Centaur; and the heedful slave
Is wander'd forth, in care to seek me out
By computation and mine host's report.
I could not speak with Dromio since at first
I sent him from the mart. See, here he comes.

The gold I gave to Dromio is being held
Safe at the Centaur; and the heedful slave
Has wandered out, in search of me
From what I gather and from the host's report.
I haven't spoken with Dromio since I first
Sent him from the mart. See, here he comes.

Enter DROMIO of Syracuse

How now sir! is your merry humour alter'd?
As you love strokes, so jest with me again.
You know no Centaur? you received no gold?
Your mistress sent to have me home to dinner?
My house was at the Phoenix? Wast thou mad,
That thus so madly thou didst answer me?

Now sir! has your merry mood changed yet?
Since you love beatings, tell me more jokes.
You know no Centaur? you received no gold?
Your mistress sent you to bring me for dinner?
My house was at the Phoenix? Were you insane,
That you would answer me with such nonsense?

DROMIO OF SYRACUSE
What answer, sir? when spake I such a word?

What answer, sir? when did I say that?

ANTIPHOLUS OF SYRACUSE
Even now, even here, not half an hour since.

Just now, right here, not half an hour ago.

DROMIO OF SYRACUSE
I did not see you since you sent me hence,
Home to the Centaur, with the gold you gave me.

I haven't seen you since you sent me away,
To go to the Centaur, with the gold you gave me.

ANTIPHOLUS OF SYRACUSE
Villain, thou didst deny the gold's receipt,
And told'st me of a mistress and a dinner;
For which, I hope, thou felt'st I was displeased.

Idiot, you denied that I gave you any gold,
And told me about a mistress and a dinner;
For which, I hope, you could tell I was upset.

DROMIO OF SYRACUSE
I am glad to see you in this merry vein:
What means this jest? I pray you, master, tell me.

I am glad to see you in this funny mood:
What does this joke mean? Please, tell me.

ANTIPHOLUS OF SYRACUSE
Yea, dost thou jeer and flout me in the teeth?
Think'st thou I jest? Hold, take thou that, and that.

You dare to laugh and mock me to my face?
You think I'm joking? Here, you, take that, and   that.

Beating him

Beating him

DROMIO OF SYRACUSE
Hold, sir, for God's sake! now your jest is earnest: Upon what bargain do you give it me?

Hold on, sir, for God's sake! now your joke is serious: What is making you behave this way?

ANTIPHOLUS OF SYRACUSE
Because that I familiarly sometimes
Do use you for my fool and chat with you,
Your sauciness will jest upon my love
And make a common of my serious hours.
When the sun shines let foolish gnats make sport,
But creep in crannies when he hides his beams.
If you will jest with me, know my aspect,
And fashion your demeanor to my looks,
Or I will beat this method in your sconce.

Because at times I act familiar with you
And laugh and joke and chat with you,
You presume to take advantage of my love
And goof around when I'm being serious.
When the sun shines foolish gnats can come out to play,
But they crawl back when he hides his beams.
If you're in a joking mood, make sure I am too,
And behave in a way that suits what I'm feeling,
Or I will beat this method into your sconce.

DROMIO OF SYRACUSE
Sconce call you it? so you would leave battering, I had rather have it a head: an you use these blows long, I must get a sconce for my head and ensconce it too; or else I shall seek my wit in my shoulders. But, I pray, sir why am I beaten?

Sconce you call it? if it will make you stop battering me, I'd call it my head: and if you keep it up, I'll need a sconce to ensconce my head;   or else my wits will be all over my shoulders. But, tell me, sir, why am I beaten?

ANTIPHOLUS OF SYRACUSE
Dost thou not know?

You mean you don't know?

DROMIO OF SYRACUSE
Nothing, sir, but that I am beaten.

All I know, sir, is that I am beaten.

ANTIPHOLUS OF SYRACUSE
Shall I tell you why?

Shall I tell you why?

DROMIO OF SYRACUSE
Ay, sir, and wherefore; for they say every why hath a wherefore.

Yes, sir, and wherefore; for they say every why has a wherefore.

ANTIPHOLUS OF SYRACUSE
Why, first,--for flouting me; and then, wherefore--
For urging it the second time to me.

Why, first,--for mocking me; and then, wherefore--
For doing it a second time again.

DROMIO OF SYRACUSE
Was there ever any man thus beaten out of season,
When in the why and the wherefore is neither rhyme nor reason?
Well, sir, I thank you.

Was there ever any man beaten like this out of season,
When in the why and the wherefore there is neither rhyme nor reason?
Well, sir, I thank you.

ANTIPHOLUS OF SYRACUSE

Thank me, sir, for what?

Thank me, sir, for what?

DROMIO OF SYRACUSE
Marry, sir, for this something that you gave me for nothing.

Well, you gave me something for   nothing.

ANTIPHOLUS OF SYRACUSE
I'll make you amends next, to give you nothing for something. But say, sir, is it dinner-time?

Next I'll make amends by giving you nothing for something. But say, sir, is it dinner-time?

DROMIO OF SYRACUSE
No, sir; I think the meat wants that I have.

No, sir; I think the meat wants that I have.

ANTIPHOLUS OF SYRACUSE
In good time, sir; what's that?

What's that?

DROMIO OF SYRACUSE
Basting.

Basting.

ANTIPHOLUS OF SYRACUSE
Well, sir, then 'twill be dry.

Well, if it's not basted it will be dry.

DROMIO OF SYRACUSE
If it be, sir, I pray you, eat none of it.

If it is, sir, I don't think you should eat it.

ANTIPHOLUS OF SYRACUSE
Your reason?

Your reason?

DROMIO OF SYRACUSE
Lest it make you choleric and purchase me another dry basting.

It might make you angry, and earn me another dry basting.

ANTIPHOLUS OF SYRACUSE

Well, sir, learn to jest in good time: there's a
time for all things.

Well, learn the appropriate time to joke: there's a
time for all things.

DROMIO OF SYRACUSE
I durst have denied that, before you were so choleric.
I would have denied that, before you were so angry.

ANTIPHOLUS OF SYRACUSE
By what rule, sir?

By what rule, sir?

DROMIO OF SYRACUSE
Marry, sir, by a rule as plain as the plain bald
pate of father Time himself.

A rule as plain as the plain bald
head of father Time himself.

ANTIPHOLUS OF SYRACUSE
Let's hear it.

Let's hear it.

DROMIO OF SYRACUSE
There's no time for a man to recover his hair that
grows bald by nature.

There's no time for a man to recover his hair that
grows bald by nature.

ANTIPHOLUS OF SYRACUSE
May he not do it by fine and recovery?

Can't he get it back by fine and recovery?

DROMIO OF SYRACUSE
Yes, to pay a fine for a periwig and recover the
lost hair of another man.

Yes, he can pay a fine for a wig and recover the
lost hair of another man.

ANTIPHOLUS OF SYRACUSE
Why is Time such a niggard of hair, being, as it is, so plentiful an excrement?

Why is Time so cheap about taking hair, being, as it is, so plentiful in growth?

DROMIO OF SYRACUSE
Because it is a blessing that he bestows on beasts; and what he hath scanted men in hair he hath
given them in wit.
Because it is a blessing that he bestows on beasts; and what he has taken from men in hair he as
given to them in wit.
ANTIPHOLUS OF SYRACUSE
Why, but there's many a man hath more hair than wit.

But there are many men with more hair than   wit.

DROMIO OF SYRACUSE
Not a man of those but he hath the wit to lose his hair.

And not one of those has had the wit to lose his hair.

ANTIPHOLUS OF SYRACUSE
Why, thou didst conclude hairy men plain dealers without wit.

So then you conclude that hairy men are simple and honest and witless.

DROMIO OF SYRACUSE
The plainer dealer, the sooner lost: yet he loseth
it in a kind of jollity.
The plainer the dealer, the sooner they lose it: yet they lose it in a kind of happiness.

ANTIPHOLUS OF SYRACUSE
For what reason?

For what reason?

DROMIO OF SYRACUSE
For two; and sound ones too.

For two reasons; and sound ones too.

ANTIPHOLUS OF SYRACUSE
Nay, not sound, I pray you.

No, don't say sound ones, please.

DROMIO OF SYRACUSE
Sure ones, then.

Sure ones, then.

ANTIPHOLUS OF SYRACUSE
Nay, not sure, in a thing falsing.

No, not sure things, since it may not be true.

DROMIO OF SYRACUSE
Certain ones then.

Certain ones then.

ANTIPHOLUS OF SYRACUSE
Name them.

Name them.

DROMIO OF SYRACUSE
The one, to save the money that he spends in
trimming; the other, that at dinner they should not drop in his porridge.

One, to save the money that he spends in
trimming his hair; Two, that at dinner the hair that falls out doesn't drop in his porridge.

ANTIPHOLUS OF SYRACUSE
You would all this time have proved there is no
time for all things.

You were supposed to have proved there is not
a time for all things.

DROMIO OF SYRACUSE
Marry, and did, sir; namely, no time to recover hair lost by nature.

Right and I did; namely, that there's no time to recover hair lost by nature.

ANTIPHOLUS OF SYRACUSE
But your reason was not substantial, why there is no time to recover.

But your reason was not substantial, why there is no time to recover.

DROMIO OF SYRACUSE
Thus I mend it: Time himself is bald and therefore to the world's end will have bald followers.
Here let me mend it with this: Time himself is bald and therefore to the world's end will have bald followers.

ANTIPHOLUS OF SYRACUSE
I knew 'twould be a bald conclusion:
But, soft! who wafts us yonder?

I knew it would be a lame conclusion:
But, wait! who's that waving to us over there?

Enter ADRIANA and LUCIANA

ADRIANA
Ay, ay, Antipholus, look strange and frown:
Some other mistress hath thy sweet aspects;
I am not Adriana nor thy wife.
The time was once when thou unurged wouldst

Yes, yes, Antipholus, look confused and frown:
Your sweet look belongs to some other mistress;
I am not Adriana nor your wife.
The time was once when without any urging you

Vow
That never words were music to thine ear,
That never object pleasing in thine eye,
That never touch well welcome to thy hand,
That never meat sweet-savor'd in thy taste,
Unless I spake, or look'd, or touch'd, or carved to thee.
How comes it now, my husband, O, how comes it,
That thou art thus estranged from thyself?
Thyself I call it, being strange to me,
That, undividable, incorporate,
Am better than thy dear self's better part.
Ah, do not tear away thyself from me!
For know, my love, as easy mayest thou fall
A drop of water in the breaking gulf,
And take unmingled that same drop again,
Without addition or diminishing,
As take from me thyself and not   me too.
How dearly would it touch me to the quick,
Shouldst thou but hear I were licentious
And that this body, consecrate to thee,
By ruffian lust should be contaminate!
Wouldst thou not spit at me and spurn at me
And hurl the name of husband in my face
And tear the stain'd skin off my harlot-brow
And from my false hand cut the wedding-ring
And break it with a deep-divorcing vow?
I know thou canst; and therefore see thou do it.
I am possess'd with an adulterate blot;
My blood is mingled with the crime of lust:
For if we too be one and thou play false,
I do digest the poison of thy flesh,
Being strumpeted by thy contagion.
Keep then far league and truce with thy true bed;
I live unstain'd, thou undishonoured.

Would swear
That never were words music to your ear,
That never an object so pleasing to your eye,
That never a touch so inviting to your hand,
That never a meat so savory to your taste,
Unless I spoke, or looked, or touched, or cooked for you.
How is it now, my husband, O, how is   it,
That you are so estranged from yourself?
I say yourself because you are strange to me,
When, imseparable, and whole,   I am better than the best part of you.
Oh, don't tear yourself away from me!
Know, my love, that as hard as it would be to
To let a drop of water fall in the breaking gulf,
And than take that same drop out again,
Without adding to it or diminishing it,
Is how it would be to take yourself away without taking me too.
How strongly it would affect me,
If you had heard that I was unfaithful
And that this body, which was promised to you,
Had been contaminated by sinful lust!
Wouldn't you spit at me, and kick me
And hurl the marriage vows in my face
And tear the branded skin off my harlot-brow
And the wedding-ring from my lying hand
And break it with a deep-divorcing vow?
I know you could; so I want to see you do it.
I am contaminated by adultery;
My blood is mingled with the crime of lust:
For if we are really one, and you have cheated,
Then you poison me as well,
Making me a whore by contagion.
Keep true, then, to your true marriage bed;
So I can live without stain, and you with honor.

ANTIPHOLUS OF SYRACUSE
Plead you to me, fair dame? I know you not:
In Ephesus I am but two hours old,
As strange unto your town as to your talk;
Who, every word by all my wit being scann'd,
Want wit in all one word to understand.

Are talking to me, pretty lady? I don't know you:
I've only been in Ephesus for two hours,
Stranger to this town and to everything you said;
I'm scanning everything you are saying,
For even one word that I can understand.

LUCIANA
Fie, brother! how the world is changed with you!
When were you wont to use my sister thus?
She sent for you by Dromio home to dinner.

For shame, brother! How you have changed!
When have you ever treated my sister like this?
She sent Dromio to bring you home to dinner.

ANTIPHOLUS OF SYRACUSE
By Dromio?

Dromio?

DROMIO OF SYRACUSE
By me?

Me?

ADRIANA
By thee; and this thou didst return from him,
That he did buffet thee, and, in his blows,
Denied my house for his, me for his wife.

Yes, you; and when you came back,
You said he beat you,
And denied that he had a house or a wife.

ANTIPHOLUS OF SYRACUSE
Did you converse, sir, with this gentlewoman?
What is the course and drift of your compact?

Did you talk to this lady?
What have you been scheming with her?

DROMIO OF SYRACUSE
I, sir? I never saw her till this time.

I, sir? I never saw her till this time.

ANTIPHOLUS OF SYRACUSE
Villain, thou liest; for even her very words
Didst thou deliver to me on the mart.

Villain, you're lying; her exact words
Are what you told me at the mart.

DROMIO OF SYRACUSE
I never spake with her in all my life.

I've never spoken to her in all my life.

ANTIPHOLUS OF SYRACUSE
How can she thus then call us by our names,
Unless it be by inspiration.

Then how does she know our names,
Unless it be by magic.

ADRIANA

How ill agrees it with your gravity
To counterfeit thus grossly with your slave,
Abetting him to thwart me in my mood!
Be it my wrong you are from me exempt,
But wrong not that wrong with a more contempt.
Come, I will fasten on this sleeve of thine:
Thou art an elm, my husband, I a vine,
Whose weakness, married to thy stronger state,
Makes me with thy strength to communicate:
If aught possess thee from me, it is dross,
Usurping ivy, brier, or idle moss;
Who, all for want of pruning, with intrusion
Infect thy sap and live on thy confusion.
It really doesn't suit a man of your rank
To lie and scheme with his slave,
To make me this upset!
It's my fault that you have wronged me,
But don't make it worse by adding contempt.
Come, I will fasten on to your sleeve:
You are an elm, my husband, I am a vine,
Whose weakness married to your strength,
Makes me strong enough to say:
If anything takes you away from me, it is trivial,
Like overgrown ivy, brier, or idle moss;
That hasn't been pruned, and whose intrusion
Infects your sap and lives to make you confused.

ANTIPHOLUS OF SYRACUSE

To me she speaks; she moves me for her theme:
What, was I married to her in my dream?
Or sleep I now and think I hear all this?
What error drives our eyes and ears amiss?
Until I know this sure uncertainty,
I'll entertain the offer'd fallacy.

She's talking to me; she means me:
What, was I married to her in my dream?
Or am I asleep now and think I hear all this?
What error is making our eyes and ears wrong?
Until I know this sure uncertainty,
I'll go along with this misconception.

LUCIANA
Dromio, go bid the servants spread for dinner.

Dromio, go get the servants ready for dinner.

DROMIO OF SYRACUSE
O, for my beads! I cross me for a sinner.
This is the fairy land: O spite of spites!
We talk with goblins, owls and sprites:
If we obey them not, this will ensue,
They'll suck our breath, or pinch us black and blue.

O, where's my rosary! I cross me for a sinner.
This is some fairy land: O spite of spites!
We talk with goblins, owls and sprites:
And if we don't obey them, they will surely,
Suck our life out, or pinch us black and   blue.

LUCIANA
Why pratest thou to thyself and answer'st not?
Dromio, thou drone, thou snail, thou slug, thou sot!

Why are you babbling to yourself instead of obeying? Dromio, you drone, you snail, you slug, you
moron!

DROMIO OF SYRACUSE
I am transformed, master, am I not?

I am transformed, master, am I not?

ANTIPHOLUS OF SYRACUSE
I think thou art in mind, and so am I.

I think your mind has been altered, as has mine

DROMIO OF SYRACUSE
Nay, master, both in mind and in my shape.

No, master, both in mind and in my shape.

ANTIPHOLUS OF SYRACUSE
Thou hast thine own form.

You still have the same form.

DROMIO OF SYRACUSE
No, I am an ape.

No, I am an ape.

LUCIANA
If thou art changed to aught, 'tis to an ass.

If you've been changed into anything, it's an ass.

DROMIO OF SYRACUSE
'Tis true; she rides me and I long for grass.
'Tis so, I am an ass; else it could never be
But I should know her as well as she knows me.

*It's true; she rides me hard and I long to be away. I must be an ass; how else could I
Not know her when she seems to know me.*

ADRIANA
Come, come, no longer will I be a fool,
To put the finger in the eye and weep,
Whilst man and master laugh my woes to scorn.
Come, sir, to dinner. Dromio, keep the gate.
Husband, I'll dine above with you to-day
And shrive you of a thousand idle pranks.
Sirrah, if any ask you for your master,
Say he dines forth, and let no creature enter.
Come, sister. Dromio, play the porter well.

*Come, come, I will not continue to be a fool,
To put a finger to my eye and weep,
While you two laugh to scorn my misery.
Come, sir, to dinner. Dromio, keep the gate.
Husband, I'll eat above with you today
And have you tell me of all your idle pranks.
Slave, if anyone asks you for your master,
Say he is eating, and let no creature enter.
Come, sister. Dromio, be a good guard.*

ANTIPHOLUS OF SYRACUSE
Am I in earth, in heaven, or in hell?
Sleeping or waking? mad or well-advised? Known unto these, and to myself disguised!
I'll say as they say and persever so,
And in this mist at all adventures go.

*Am I in earth, in heaven, or in hell?
Sleeping or waking? Sane or insane?*   *Known to these people, but not to myself!*
*I'll just have to keep up the pretence,
And persevere as long as I can.*

DROMIO OF SYRACUSE
Master, shall I be porter at the gate?

Master, should I still guard the gate?

ADRIANA
Ay; and let none enter, lest I break your pate.

Yes; and let none enter, or else I'll break your head.

LUCIANA
Come, come, Antipholus, we dine too late.

Come, come, Antipholus, it's already getting late.

Exeunt

Act 3

SCENE I. Before the house of ANTIPHOLUS of Ephesus.

Enter ANTIPHOLUS of Ephesus, DROMIO of Ephesus, ANGELO, and BALTHAZAR

ANTIPHOLUS OF EPHESUS
Good Signior Angelo, you must excuse us all;
My wife is shrewish when I keep not hours:
Say that I linger'd with you at your shop
To see the making of her carcanet,
And that to-morrow you will bring it home.
But here's a villain that would face me down
He met me on the mart, and that I beat him,
And charged him with a thousand marks in gold,
And that I did deny my wife and house.
Thou drunkard, thou, what didst thou mean by this?

Mister Angelo, you must excuse us all;
My wife nags me when I don't watch the time:
Say that I lingered with you at your shop
To see the making of her necklace,
And that tomorrow you will bring it home.
But here's a moron that has been telling lies
That he met me at the mart, and that I beat him,
And charged him with a thousand marks in gold,
And that I denied that I had a wife and house.
You stupid drunkard, what was the meaning of all that?

DROMIO OF EPHESUS
Say what you will, sir, but I know what I know;
That you beat me at the mart, I have your hand to show:
If the skin were parchment, and the blows you gave were ink,
Your own handwriting would tell you what I think.

Say what you will, sir, but I know what I know;
That you beat me at the mart, I have the bruises to prove it:
If skin was parchment, and your punches were ink,
Your own handwriting would tell you the same I think.

ANTIPHOLUS OF EPHESUS
I think thou art an ass.

I think you're an ass.

DROMIO OF EPHESUS
Marry, so it doth appear
By the wrongs I suffer and the blows I bear.
I should kick, being kick'd; and, being at that pass,
You would keep from my heels and beware of an ass.

Well, it sure seems that way, what with all the wrongs I suffer and the bruises I bear.
I should kick back when I'm kicked; if I really am a mule,
You would be scared of my kicks and keep away.

ANTIPHOLUS OF EPHESUS
You're sad, Signior Balthazar: pray God our cheer
May answer my good will and your good welcome here.

You're sad, Mister Balthazar: I hope that you will cheer up
Because of my good will towards you, and know how welcome you are here.

BALTHAZAR
I hold your dainties cheap, sir, and your
welcome dear.

Your dainties mean far less to me than your welcome, I'm grateful.

ANTIPHOLUS OF EPHESUS
O, Signior Balthazar, either at flesh or fish,
A table full of welcome make scarce one dainty dish.

O, Mister Balthazar, whether it's meat or fish,
A table full of welcome is far better than a dainty dish.

BALTHAZAR
Good meat, sir, is common; that every churl affords.

Good meat, sir, is common; every peasant can afford that.

ANTIPHOLUS OF EPHESUS
And welcome more common; for that's nothing but words.

And welcome is even more common than that; for that's nothing but words.

BALTHAZAR
Small cheer and great welcome makes a merry feast.

Little food with a great welcome makes a merry feast.

ANTIPHOLUS OF EPHESUS
Ay, to a niggardly host, and more sparing guest:
But though my cates be mean, take them in good part;
Better cheer may you have, but not with better heart.
But, soft! my door is lock'd. Go bid them let us in.

Yes, to a cheap host, and cheaper guest:
But even if my food is not good, eat it with my good intent;
There may be better food elsewhere, but not with better heart.
But, what's this! my door is locked. Go bid them let us in.

DROMIO OF EPHESUS
Maud, Bridget, Marian, Cicel, Gillian, Ginn!

Maud, Bridget, Marian, Cicel, Gillian, Ginn!

DROMIO OF SYRACUSE
[Within] Mome, malt-horse, capon, coxcomb,
idiot, patch!
Either get thee from the door, or sit down at the hatch.
Dost thou conjure for wenches, that thou call'st
for such store,
When one is one too many? Go, get thee from the door.

[Within] Blockhead, stupid, moron, fool,
idiot, clown!
Either get away from the door, or sit down at the gate.
Are you conjuring whores, is that why you're shouting so many names,
Is your one not enough? Go, get away from the door.

DROMIO OF EPHESUS
What patch is made our porter? My master stays in the street.

What clown has been made our guard? My master is standing in the street.

DROMIO OF SYRACUSE
[Within] Let him walk from whence he came, lest he catch cold on's feet.

[Within] Let him walk back to where he came, or he'll catch cold.

ANTIPHOLUS OF EPHESUS
Who talks within there? ho, open the door!

Who's talking in there? hey, open the door!

DROMIO OF SYRACUSE
[Within] Right, sir; I'll tell you when, an you tell
me wherefore.

[Within] Right, sir; I'll tell you if I'll open it if you tell me why I should.

ANTIPHOLUS OF EPHESUS
Wherefore? for my dinner: I have not dined to-day.

Why? for my dinner: I have not eaten yet   today.

DROMIO OF SYRACUSE
[Within] Nor to-day here you must not; come again when you may.

[Within] And you won't eat here either; come again some other time.

ANTIPHOLUS OF EPHESUS
What art thou that keepest me out from the house I owe?

Who are you to keep me out of my own house?

DROMIO OF SYRACUSE
[Within] The porter for this time, sir, and my name is Dromio.

[Within] I'm the guard for today, sir, and my name is Dromio.

DROMIO OF EPHESUS
O villain! thou hast stolen both mine office and my name.
The one ne'er got me credit, the other mickle blame.
If thou hadst been Dromio to-day in my place,
Thou wouldst have changed thy face for a name or thy name for an ass.

You jerk! you have stolen both my job and my name.
Though I never get credit for one, and the other only gets me blame.
If you had been Dromio in my place today,
You would have had your face changed to a target, and your name changed to "ass."

LUCE
[Within] What a coil is there, Dromio? who are those at the gate?

[Within] What's the confusion out there, Dromio? who are the people at the gate?

DROMIO OF EPHESUS
Let my master in, Luce.

Let my master in, Luce.

LUCE
[Within] Faith, no; he comes too late;
And so tell your master.

[Within] No way; he comes too late;
Tell your master that.

DROMIO OF EPHESUS
O Lord, I must laugh!
Have at you with a proverb--Shall I set in my staff?

O Lord, this is too funny!
I'll fire back with a proverb—May I make myself at home?

LUCE
[Within] Have at you with another; that's--When? can you tell?

[Within] I'll fire back at you with another; that's—I'd like to see you try.

DROMIO OF SYRACUSE
[Within] If thy name be call'd Luce--Luce, thou hast answered him well.

[Within] If you're the one called Luce--Luce, nice comeback.

ANTIPHOLUS OF EPHESUS
Do you hear, you minion? you'll let us in, I hope?

Can you hear me, you slave? You're going to let us in, right?

LUCE
[Within] I thought to have asked you.

[Within] I thought I asked you that.

DROMIO OF SYRACUSE
[Within] And you said no.

[Within] And you said no.

DROMIO OF EPHESUS
So, come, help: well struck! there was blow for blow.

Some one help me bang on the door: nice hit! That was blow for blow.

ANTIPHOLUS OF EPHESUS
Thou baggage, let me in.

You useless idiot, let me in.

LUCE
[Within] Can you tell for whose sake?

[Within] Says who?

DROMIO OF EPHESUS
Master, knock the door hard.

Master, knock the door hard.

LUCE
[Within] Let him knock till it ache.

[Within] Let him knock till he aches.

ANTIPHOLUS OF EPHESUS
You'll cry for this, minion, if I beat the door down.

You'll pay for this, slave, even if I have to beat the door down.

LUCE
[Within] What needs all that, and a pair of stocks in the town?

[Within] What are we wasting all this time for? There's a pair of stocks in the town.

ADRIANA
[Within] Who is that at the door that keeps all
this noise?

[Within] Who is making all of this noise at the door?

DROMIO OF SYRACUSE
[Within] By my troth, your town is troubled with
unruly boys.

*[Within] I swear, your town is troubled with
unruly boys.*

ANTIPHOLUS OF EPHESUS
Are you there, wife? you might have come before.

Is that you, wife? you should have come much sooner.

ADRIANA
[Within] Your wife, sir knave! go get you from the door.

[Within] Your wife, stupid! go on get out of here.

DROMIO OF EPHESUS
If you went in pain, master, this 'knave' would go sore.

If you get punished, master, I'm going to get it even worse.

ANGELO
Here is neither cheer, sir, nor welcome: we would fain have either.

There seems to be no food here, sir, nor welcome: looks like we won't be getting any.

BALTHAZAR
In debating which was best, we shall part with neither.

BALTHAZAR
And after all that talk of which was best, we'll have to leave without either.

DROMIO OF EPHESUS
They stand at the door, master; bid them welcome hither.

They are just standing at the door, master; tell them they are welcome here.

ANTIPHOLUS OF EPHESUS
There is something in the wind, that we cannot get in.

There is something strange in the wind that is keeping us from getting in.

DROMIO OF EPHESUS
You would say so, master, if your garments were thin.
Your cake there is warm within; you stand here in the cold:
It would make a man mad as a buck, to be so bought and sold.

You'd definitely be saying that, master, if your clothes were as thin as mine.
The food inside is warm; you stand here in the cold:
It would make another man mad as a buck, to be betrayed like this.

ANTIPHOLUS OF EPHESUS
Go fetch me something: I'll break ope the gate.

Go fetch me something: I'll break open the gate.

DROMIO OF SYRACUSE
[Within] Break any breaking here, and I'll break your knave's pate.

[Within] Break anything here, and I'll break your fool's head in.

DROMIO OF EPHESUS
A man may break a word with you, sir, and words are but wind,
Ay, and break it in your face, so he break it not behind.

A man may break words with you, sir, and words are only wind,
So, get ready for me to break wind right in your face.

DROMIO OF SYRACUSE
[Within] It seems thou want'st breaking: out upon thee, hind!

[Within] You're just begging to be broken: scram, you dog!

DROMIO OF EPHESUS
Here's too much 'out upon thee!' I pray thee,
let me in.

I sick of all this 'scram! get out!' Come on, please, let me in.

DROMIO OF SYRACUSE
[Within] Ay, when fowls have no feathers and fish have no fin.

DROMIO OF SYRACUSE
[Within] Sure, when birds have no feathers and fish have no fins.

ANTIPHOLUS OF EPHESUS
Well, I'll break in: go borrow me a crow.

ANTIPHOLUS OF EPHESUS
Well, I'll break in: go find me a crow.

DROMIO OF EPHESUS
A crow without feather? Master, mean you so?
For a fish without a fin, there's a fowl without a feather;
If a crow help us in, sirrah, we'll pluck a crow together.

DROMIO OF EPHESUS
You mean a crow without feathers? For real?
To prove that there's fish without fins and birds without feathers;
If that's what it takes to get in, you dirty slave, you and I will have a score to settle.

ANTIPHOLUS OF EPHESUS
Go get thee gone; fetch me an iron crow.

No, idiot, go and get me a crowbar.

BALTHAZAR
Have patience, sir; O, let it not be so!
Herein you war against your reputation
And draw within the compass of suspect
The unviolated honour of your wife.
Once this,--your long experience of her wisdom,
Her sober virtue, years and modesty,
Plead on her part some cause to you unknown:
And doubt not, sir, but she will well excuse
Why at this time the doors are made against you.
Be ruled by me: depart in patience,
And let us to the Tiger all to dinner,
And about evening come yourself alone
To know the reason of this strange restraint.
If by strong hand you offer to break in
Now in the stirring passage of the day,
A vulgar comment will be made of it,
And that supposed by the common rout
Against your yet ungalled estimation
That may with foul intrusion enter in
And dwell upon your grave when you are dead;
For slander lives upon succession,
For ever housed where it gets possession.

Have patience, sir; O, please don't do this!
You're going to ruin your reputation
And bring your wife into suspicion
Though her honor is as of yet untarnished.
Listen— you have a lot of experience with her,
Her wisdom, virtues, maturity and modesty,   She must have a reason that you don't know:
Do not doubt that she will explain later
Why your doors are closed to you.
Take my advice: let's just leave patiently,
And all go out to the Tiger for dinner,
And when evening falls you come back alone
To find out the reason for this strange lockout.
If you threaten brute force to break in
Now when everyone is out about town,
Someone will see and make a vulgar comment,
And the common people will make assumptions
Against your currently flawless reputation
That may end up contaminating
And defiling your grave when you are dead;
Since slander lives through succession,
and will stay with your family forever.

ANTIPHOLUS OF EPHESUS
You have prevailed: I will depart in quiet,
And, in despite of mirth, mean to be merry.
I know a wench of excellent discourse,
Pretty and witty; wild, and yet, too, gentle:
There will we dine. This woman that I mean,
My wife--but, I protest, without desert--
Hath oftentimes upbraided me withal:
To her will we to dinner.

You win: I will leave quietly,
And, though I'm upset I'll try to be happy.
I know a wench with charming conversation,
Pretty and witty; wild, but also gentle:
We'll dine with her. This woman,
My wife—even though I deny it to no avail--
has often accused me of being unfaithful with:
We will go dine with her.

To Angelo

To Angelo

Get you home
And fetch the chain; by this I know 'tis made:
Bring it, I pray you, to the Porpentine;
For there's the house: that chain will I bestow--
Be it for nothing but to spite my wife--
Upon mine hostess there: good sir, make haste.
Since mine own doors refuse to entertain me,
I'll knock elsewhere, to see if they'll disdain me.

Go to your house
And fetch the chain; by now I know it's done:
Bring it, please, to the Porpentine;
That's where she is: I'll give the chain—   Just to spite my wife--
To the hostess there: go quickly, good sir.
Since my own doors are closed to me,
I'll knock elsewhere and see if they turn me away.

ANGELO
I'll meet you at that place some hour hence.

ANGELO
I'll meet you at that place in about an hour.

ANTIPHOLUS OF EPHESUS
Do so. This jest shall cost me some expense.

Do it. This prank is going to be expensive.

Exeunt

SCENE II. The same.

Enter LUCIANA and ANTIPHOLUS of Syracuse

LUCIANA
And may it be that you have quite forgot
A husband's office? shall, Antipholus.
Even in the spring of love, thy love-springs rot?
Shall love, in building, grow so ruinous?
If you did wed my sister for her wealth,
Then for her wealth's sake use her with more kindness:
Or if you like elsewhere, do it by stealth;
Muffle your false love with some show of blindness:
Let not my sister read it in your eye;
Be not thy tongue thy own shame's orator;
Look sweet, be fair, become disloyalty;
Apparel vice like virtue's harbinger;
Bear a fair presence, though your heart be tainted;
Teach sin the carriage of a holy saint;
Be secret-false: what need she be acquainted?
What simple thief brags of his own attaint?
'Tis double wrong, to truant with your bed
And let her read it in thy looks at board:
Shame hath a bastard fame, well managed;
Ill deeds are doubled with an evil word.
Alas, poor women! make us but believe,
Being compact of credit, that you love us;
Though others have the arm, show us the sleeve;
We in your motion turn and you may move us.
Then, gentle brother, get you in again;
Comfort my sister, cheer her, call her wife:
'Tis holy sport to be a little vain,
When the sweet breath of flattery conquers strife.

Could it be that you have completely forgotten
A husband's duties? Will you, Antipholus.
Even in the spring of your love, let it rot?
Will your love be ruined as it grows?
If you married my sister for her money,
Then even just for her money treat her better than this:
Or if you are seeing someone else, be stealthy;
Muffle your false love by acting like you are blind and ignorant:
Don't let my sister see it in your eyes;
Don't let your tongue tell your shame;
Look sweet, be kind, make disloyalty look good;
Make your misconduct look virtuous;
At least act like you are a good person, though your heart is tainted;
Teach your sin to look holy;
Be secretive, lie: why does she have to know?
Does a simple thief brag of the things he stole?
It's twice as bad, to be unfaithful to your wife And then to let her see it on your face:
Shame's bastard is fame, which can be managed;
Bad deeds are made worse by speaking of them.
Alas, poor women! we believe when you say,
being so trusting, that you love us;
You have someone else on your arm, and we get the sleeve; we move however you want.
So, gentle brother, please come to your senses;
Comfort my sister, cheer her, call her wife:
It can be holy to lie,
If it's a sweet lie that hides an awful truth.

ANTIPHOLUS OF SYRACUSE

Sweet mistress--what your name is else, I know not,
Nor by what wonder you do hit of mine,--
Less in your knowledge and your grace you show not
Than our earth's wonder, more than earth divine.
Teach me, dear creature, how to think and speak;
Lay open to my earthy-gross conceit,
Smother'd in errors, feeble, shallow, weak,
The folded meaning of your words' deceit.
Against my soul's pure truth why labour you
To make it wander in an unknown field?
Are you a god? would you create me new?
Transform me then, and to your power I'll yield.
But if that I am I, then well I know
Your weeping sister is no wife of mine,
Nor to her bed no homage do I owe

Sweet mistress—I don't know what else to call you,
Or how you seem to know my name,--
You have more knowledge and are more graceful
Than the earth is wonderful and divine.
Teach me, dear creature, how to think and speak;
Show me in my vain and flawed understanding,
Covered in errors, feeble, shallow, weak,
The hidden meaning behind your words.
Against my soul's pure truth why are you trying
To make it wander in an unknown field?
Are you a god? are you recreating me?
Transform me then, I'll yield to your power.
But if I am really me, then I know very well
Your weeping sister is no wife of mine,
Nor do I owe any homage to her bed
Far more, far more to you do I decline.
O, train me not, sweet mermaid, with thy note,
To drown me in thy sister's flood of tears:
Sing, siren, for thyself and I will dote:
Spread o'er the silver waves thy golden hairs,
And as a bed I'll take them and there lie,
And in that glorious supposition think
He gains by death that hath such means to die:
Let Love, being light, be drowned if she sink!
I am far, far more inclined towards you.
O, don't make me, sweet mermaid, with your song, drown in your sister's flood of tears:
Sing, siren, for me to choose you and I will:
Spread your golden hairs over the silver waves,
And I will lie on them like a bed,
And in that glorious position think
That any man would be lucky to die there:
Let Love, being truth, be drowned if I lie!

LUCIANA
What, are you mad, that you do reason so?
What, have you gone crazy, talking like this?
ANTIPHOLUS OF SYRACUSE
Not mad, but mated; how, I do not know.
Not crazy, but in love; I don't know how.

LUCIANA
It is a fault that springeth from your eye.
It is your eyes playing tricks on you.

ANTIPHOLUS OF SYRACUSE
For gazing on your beams, fair sun, being by.
From gazing at you, shining like the sun.

LUCIANA
Gaze where you should, and that will clear your sight.
Gaze where you're supposed to, and that will clear your sight.
ANTIPHOLUS OF SYRACUSE
As good to wink, sweet love, as look on night.
I would rather close my eyes, sweet love, than look at the darkness of night.

LUCIANA
Why call you me love? call my sister so.
Why do you call me "love"? call my sister that.
ANTIPHOLUS OF SYRACUSE
Thy sister's sister.
Your sister's sister.

LUCIANA
That's my sister.
That's my sister.
ANTIPHOLUS OF SYRACUSE
No;
It is thyself, mine own self's better part,
Mine eye's clear eye, my dear heart's dearer heart,
My food, my fortune and my sweet hope's aim,
My sole earth's heaven and my heaven's claim.
No;
It is you, my own self's better half,
My clearer eye, my heart's love,
My food, my fortune and my dearest dream,
My heaven on this earth, and my key to heaven.

LUCIANA
All this my sister is, or else should be.
My sister is all of that, or she should be.

ANTIPHOLUS OF SYRACUSE
Call thyself sister, sweet, for I am thee.
Thee will I love and with thee lead my life:
Thou hast no husband yet nor I no wife.
Give me thy hand.
Call yourself sister, sweet, for I am you.
I love you, I want to spend my life with you:
You have no husband yet, I have no wife.
Marry me.

LUCIANA
O, soft, air! hold you still:
I'll fetch my sister, to get her good will.
O, stop, sir! just stay right there:
I'll go get my sister, to see what she says.
Exit

Enter DROMIO of Syracuse

ANTIPHOLUS OF SYRACUSE
Why, how now, Dromio! where runn'st thou so fast?
Why, what's this, Dromio! where are you running so fast?

DROMIO OF SYRACUSE
Do you know me, sir? am I Dromio? am I your man? am I myself?
Do you know me, sir? am I Dromio? am I your servant? am I myself?
ANTIPHOLUS OF SYRACUSE
Thou art Dromio, thou art my man, thou art thyself.
You are Dromio, you are my servant, you are yourself.
DROMIO OF SYRACUSE
I am an ass, I am a woman's man and besides myself.
I am an ass, I am a woman's servant and beside myself.

ANTIPHOLUS OF SYRACUSE
What woman's man? and how besides thyself? besides thyself?
What woman's servant? and what do you mean beside yourself? Besides yourself?

DROMIO OF SYRACUSE
Marry, sir, besides myself, I am due to a woman; one that claims me, one that haunts me, one that will have me.
Yes, sir, beside myself, I am servant to a woman; one that claims me, one that haunts me, one that will have me.

ANTIPHOLUS OF SYRACUSE
What claim lays she to thee?
What claim does she have on you?

DROMIO OF SYRACUSE
Marry sir, such claim as you would lay to your
horse; and she would have me as a beast: not that, I
being a beast, she would have me; but that she,
being a very beastly creature, lays claim to me.
The same kind of claim you have on your
horse; she wants me like a beast: I don't mean That if I was an animal, she would have me; I Mean
that she, being a very beastly creature, wants to claim me.
ANTIPHOLUS OF SYRACUSE
What is she?
What is she?

DROMIO OF SYRACUSE
A very reverent body; ay, such a one as a man may not speak of without he say 'Sir-reverence.' I
have but lean luck in the match, and yet is she a
wondrous fat marriage.
A very momentous person; so weighty a person That before speaking to her one must first say
'Excuse me.' I have had very thin luck with her, and yet she is a ponderously fat marriage.
ANTIPHOLUS OF SYRACUSE
How dost thou mean a fat marriage?
What do you mean a fat marriage?

DROMIO OF SYRACUSE
Marry, sir, she's the kitchen wench and all grease;
and I know not what use to put her to but to make a lamp of her and run from her by her own light.
I warrant, her rags and the tallow in them will burn a Poland winter: if she lives till doomsday,
she'll burn a week longer than the whole world.
Well, sir, she's the kitchen wench, so she's all greasy;
and I don't know what use she is except to make a lamp from all her grease so I can run away by
the light of it. She's so oily I bet she could burn through a Poland winter: if she lives till
doomsday, she'll burn a week longer than the whole world.
ANTIPHOLUS OF SYRACUSE
What complexion is she of?
What complexion is she of?

DROMIO OF SYRACUSE
Swart, like my shoe, but her face nothing half so
clean kept: for why, she sweats; a man may go over shoes in the grime of it.
Dark, like my shoe, but nowhere near as clean: because she sweats; you could be ankle deep in the
grime of it.

ANTIPHOLUS OF SYRACUSE
That's a fault that water will mend.
That's nothing a little water couldn't fix.

DROMIO OF SYRACUSE
No, sir, 'tis in grain; Noah's flood could not do it.
No, it's ingrained; Noah's flood couldn't do it.
ANTIPHOLUS OF SYRACUSE
What's her name?
What's her name?

DROMIO OF SYRACUSE
Nell, sir; but her name and three quarters, that's
an ell and three quarters, will not measure her from hip to hip.
Nell, sir; but her name and three quarters, that's
an ell and three quarters, won't even cover the distance from one of her hips to the other.
ANTIPHOLUS OF SYRACUSE
Then she bears some breadth?
Then she must be wide?

DROMIO OF SYRACUSE
No longer from head to foot than from hip to hip:
she is spherical, like a globe; I could find out
countries in her.
She's the same head to toe as hip to hip:
she is spherical, like a globe; I could find out where countries are by using her.
ANTIPHOLUS OF SYRACUSE
In what part of her body stands Ireland?
Where would Ireland be on her?

DROMIO OF SYRACUSE
Marry, in her buttocks: I found it out by the bogs.
In her buttocks: I found it because that's where it's boggiest.
ANTIPHOLUS OF SYRACUSE
Where Scotland?
Where would Scotland be?

DROMIO OF SYRACUSE
I found it by the barrenness; hard in the palm of the hand.
I found it where it's hard and empty; the calloused palm of her hand.
ANTIPHOLUS OF SYRACUSE
Where France?
Where is France?

DROMIO OF SYRACUSE
In her forehead; armed and reverted, making war
against her heir.
In her forehead; her receding hairline, making war against her heir.
ANTIPHOLUS OF SYRACUSE
Where England?
Where is England?

DROMIO OF SYRACUSE
I looked for the chalky cliffs, but I could find no
whiteness in them; but I guess it stood in her chin,
by the salt rheum that ran between France and it.
I looked for chalky cliffs, but her teeth weren't white enough; So I guess it would be her chin,
Because of the slimy sweat on her face between it and France.
ANTIPHOLUS OF SYRACUSE
Where Spain?
Where is Spain?

DROMIO OF SYRACUSE
Faith, I saw it not; but I felt it hot in her breath.
Honestly, I didn't see it; I felt it in her hot breath.
ANTIPHOLUS OF SYRACUSE
Where America, the Indies?
Where is America, the Indies?

DROMIO OF SYRACUSE
Oh, sir, upon her nose all o'er embellished with
rubies, carbuncles, sapphires, declining their rich
aspect to the hot breath of Spain; who sent whole
armadoes of caracks to be ballast at her nose.
Oh, sir, all over her nose, it was covered
With pimples, sores and welts, melting
Down to the hot breath of Spain; who sent its
Own forces to plug up her nose.
ANTIPHOLUS OF SYRACUSE
Where stood Belgia, the Netherlands?
Where was Belgium, the Netherlands?

DROMIO OF SYRACUSE
Oh, sir, I did not look so low. To conclude, this
drudge, or diviner, laid claim to me, call'd me
Dromio; swore I was assured to her; told me what privy marks I had about me, as, the mark of my
shoulder, the mole in my neck, the great wart on my left arm, that I amazed ran from her as a
witch:
And, I think, if my breast had not been made of
faith and my heart of steel,
She had transform'd me to a curtal dog and made
me turn i' the wheel.
Oh, sir, I did not look so low. To conclude, this
Peasant witch, claimed I was hers, called me
Dromio; swore I was promised to her; told me What birth marks I had, like the one on my
shoulder, the mole on my neck, the great wart on my left arm, and I was so shocked that I ran from
the witch:
And, I think, if my chest hadn't been so brave or my heart so strong,
She would have transformed me into her dog and made me her slave.
ANTIPHOLUS OF SYRACUSE
Go hie thee presently, post to the road:
An if the wind blow any way from shore,
I will not harbour in this town to-night:
If any bark put forth, come to the mart,
Go quickly, keep watch on the road:
If the wind is blowing away from shore,
I will not sleep in this town tonight:
If any ship sets out, come to the mart,

Where I will walk till thou return to me.
If every one knows us and we know none,
'Tis time, I think, to trudge, pack and be gone.
Where I will be waiting for you.
If every one knows us and we know no one,
Then I think it's time to get our things and leave.

DROMIO OF SYRACUSE
As from a bear a man would run for life,
So fly I from her that would be my wife.
Like a man would for his life from a bear,   *I'll run from the woman who wants to be my wife.*
Exit

ANTIPHOLUS OF SYRACUSE
There's none but witches do inhabit here;
And therefore 'tis high time that I were hence.
She that doth call me husband, even my soul
Doth for a wife abhor. But her fair sister,
Possess'd with such a gentle sovereign grace,
Of such enchanting presence and discourse,
Hath almost made me traitor to myself:
But, lest myself be guilty to self-wrong,
I'll stop mine ears against the mermaid's song.
Apparently only witches live here;
Which means it's high time I left.
That lady who calls me husband, my very soul
Couldn't stand for a wife. But her fair sister,
Who is so graceful, and gentle and lovely,
Whose presence and conversation enchant me,
Has almost made me reveal my identity:
But unless I want to betray myself,
I better stop up my ears to her mermaid's song.

Enter ANGELO with the chain

ANGELO
Master Antipholus,--
Master Antipholus,--

ANTIPHOLUS OF SYRACUSE
Ay, that's my name.
Yes, that's my name.

ANGELO
I know it well, sir, lo, here is the chain.
I thought to have ta'en you at the Porpentine:
The chain unfinish'd made me stay thus long.
I know very well, sir, here, here is the chain.
I was going to take it to you at the Porpentine:
But it took me a long time to finish it.
ANTIPHOLUS OF SYRACUSE
What is your will that I shall do with this?
What would you like me to do with this?

ANGELO
What please yourself, sir: I have made it for you.
Whatever you want, sir: I have made it for you.

ANTIPHOLUS OF SYRACUSE
Made it for me, sir! I bespoke it not.
Made it for me, sir? I didn't order this.

ANGELO
Not once, nor twice, but twenty times you have.
Go home with it and please your wife withal;
And soon at supper-time I'll visit you
And then receive my money for the chain.
Not once, or twice, but twenty times you have.
Go home, use it to make your wife happy;
And soon at supper-time I'll visit you
And then you can pay me then for it.
ANTIPHOLUS OF SYRACUSE
I pray you, sir, receive the money now,
For fear you ne'er see chain nor money more.
Please, sir, let me pay you now,
Otherwise you may never see the chain or
money.

ANGELO
You are a merry man, sir: fare you well.
You are one funny man, sir: goodbye.
Exit

ANTIPHOLUS OF SYRACUSE
What I should think of this, I cannot tell:
But this I think, there's no man is so vain
That would refuse so fair an offer'd chain.
I see a man here needs not live by shifts,
When in the streets he meets such golden gifts.
I'll to the mart, and there for Dromio stay
If any ship put out, then straight away.
I have no idea what to think of this:
But I do think, that no man is too proud
To refuse such a beautiful chain that is offered.
It seems like a man here doesn't have to steal,
When people are giving away gold in the streets.
I'll go to the mart and wait for Dromio
And if he says there's a ship leaving tonight then We will set out immediately.

Exit

Act 4

SCENE I. A public place.

Enter Second Merchant, ANGELO, and an Officer

SECOND MERCHANT
You know since Pentecost the sum is due,
And since I have not much importuned you;
Nor now I had not, but that I am bound
To Persia, and want guilders for my voyage:
Therefore make present satisfaction,
Or I'll attach you by this officer.
You know you've owed me since Pentecost,
And I haven't been pestering you for it;
And I wouldn't now but I have to,
I need money for my voyage to Persia:
So you must pay me back now,
Or I'll have this officer arrest you.

ANGELO
Even just the sum that I do owe to you
Is growing to me by Antipholus,
And in the instant that I met with you
He had of me a chain: at five o'clock
I shall receive the money for the same.
Pleaseth you walk with me down to his house,
I will discharge my bond and thank you too.
The exact amount that I owe you
Is how much I am about to get from Antipholus,
Right before I met you
I gave him a chain: at five o'clock
He's going to pay me for it.
If you would like to walk with me to his house,
I will gladly pay you back.

Enter ANTIPHOLUS of Ephesus and DROMIO of Ephesus from the courtezan's

OFFICER
That labour may you save: see where he comes.
You don't have to walk: there he is.
ANTIPHOLUS OF EPHESUS
While I go to the goldsmith's house, go thou
And buy a rope's end: that will I bestow
Among my wife and her confederates,
For locking me out of my doors by day.
But, soft! I see the goldsmith. Get thee gone;
Buy thou a rope and bring it home to me.
While I go to the goldsmith's house, you go
And buy a piece of rope: I'll use it to whip
My wife and her comrades,
For locking me out of my house today.
But, wait! I see the goldsmith. Get out of here;
Go buy a rope and bring it home to me.

DROMIO OF EPHESUS
I buy a thousand pound a year: I buy a rope.
I buy myself a thousand beatings by buying rope.
Exit

ANTIPHOLUS OF EPHESUS
A man is well holp up that trusts to you:
I promised your presence and the chain;
But neither chain nor goldsmith came to me.
Belike you thought our love would last too long,
If it were chain'd together, and therefore came not.
Some good it does a man to trust you:
I promised that you would come with the chain;
But neither you nor the chain ever came.
Maybe you thought our love would last longer,
If it were chained together, and so you decided not to come.

ANGELO

Saving your merry humour, here's the note
How much your chain weighs to the utmost carat,
The fineness of the gold and chargeful fashion.
Which doth amount to three odd ducats more
Than I stand debted to this gentleman:
Save your jokes, here's the bill for
How much your chain weighs to the last carat,
The fineness of the gold and expensive design.
Which amounts to about three more ducats
Than I already owe to this gentleman:

I pray you, see him presently discharged,
For he is bound to sea and stays but for it.
If you would, please, pay him now,
Since he's leaving and can't set sail without it.
ANTIPHOLUS OF EPHESUS

I am not furnish'd with the present money;
Besides, I have some business in the town.
Good signior, take the stranger to my house
And with you take the chain and bid my wife
Disburse the sum on the receipt thereof:
Perchance I will be there as soon as you.
I don't have the money on me at the moment;
Besides, I have some business in the town.
Good sir, please take the stranger to my house
And take the chain with you, ask my wife
To give you the money when she gets the chain:
I may be there shortly.

ANGELO

Then you will bring the chain to her yourself?
Then you will bring the chain to her yourself?
ANTIPHOLUS OF EPHESUS

No; bear it with you, lest I come not time enough.
No; take it with you in case I don't come home in time.

ANGELO

Well, sir, I will. Have you the chain about you?
Well, sir, sounds good. Do you have it with you?

ANTIPHOLUS OF EPHESUS
An if I have not, sir, I hope you have;
Or else you may return without your money.
If I don't have it, sir, I hope you do;
Or else you may return without your money.

ANGELO
Nay, come, I pray you, sir, give me the chain:
Both wind and tide stays for this gentleman,
And I, to blame, have held him here too long.
No, come on, please, give me the chain:
Both wind and tide wait for this gentleman,
And it's my fault for keeping him so long.

ANTIPHOLUS OF EPHESUS
Good Lord! you use this dalliance to excuse
Your breach of promise to the Porpentine.
I should have chid you for not bringing it,
But, like a shrew, you first begin to brawl.
Good Lord! you're using this trifling matter
To excuse breaking your promise to meet us.
I should have scolded you for not bringing it,
But, like a shrew, you started fighting me first.

SECOND MERCHANT
The hour steals on; I pray you, sir, dispatch.
It's really getting late; please, sir, the payment.

ANGELO
You hear how he importunes me;--the chain!
You hear how bothersome he is;--the chain!

ANTIPHOLUS OF EPHESUS
Why, give it to my wife and fetch your money.
Well, give it to my wife and get your money.

ANGELO
Come, come, you know I gave it you even now.
Either send the chain or send me by some token.
Come on, you know I gave it to you just now.
Either give me the chain or give me the money.

ANTIPHOLUS OF EPHESUS
Fie, now you run this humour out of breath,
where's the chain? I pray you, let me see it.
Wow, now you're getting on my nerves,
where's the chain? Come on, let me see it.

SECOND MERCHANT
My business cannot brook this dalliance.
Good sir, say whether you'll answer me or no:
If not, I'll leave him to the officer.
I'm far too busy for this nonsense.
Good sir, say whether you'll answer me or not:
If not, I'll leave him to the officer.
ANTIPHOLUS OF EPHESUS
I answer you! what should I answer you?
I answer you! what should I answer you?

ANGELO
The money that you owe me for the chain.
The money that you owe me for the chain.
ANTIPHOLUS OF EPHESUS
I owe you none till I receive the chain.
I owe you nothing till I receive the chain.

ANGELO
You know I gave it you half an hour since.
You know I gave it you half an hour ago.
ANTIPHOLUS OF EPHESUS
You gave me none: you wrong me much to say so.
You gave me nothing: you wrong me much by saying so.

ANGELO
You wrong me more, sir, in denying it:
Consider how it stands upon my credit.
You wrong me more, sir, in denying it:
Consider how bad this makes me look.

SECOND MERCHANT
Well, officer, arrest him at my suit.
Well, officer, arrest him for not paying.

OFFICER
I do; and charge you in the duke's name to obey me.
I am; and charge you in the duke's name to obey me.

ANGELO
This touches me in reputation.
Either consent to pay this sum for me
Or I attach you by this officer.
This is so bad for my reputation.
Either consent to pay this debt for me
Or I'll have this officer arrest you.
ANTIPHOLUS OF EPHESUS
Consent to pay thee that I never had!
Arrest me, foolish fellow, if thou darest.
Consent to pay you for something I don't have!
Arrest me, stupid man, if you dare.

ANGELO
Here is thy fee; arrest him, officer,
I would not spare my brother in this case,
If he should scorn me so apparently.
Here is your fee; arrest him, officer,
I would not spare even my brother in this case,
If he scorned me so openly in public.

OFFICER
I do arrest you, sir: you hear the suit.
I do arrest you, sir: you hear the charge.
ANTIPHOLUS OF EPHESUS
I do obey thee till I give thee bail.
But, sirrah, you shall buy this sport as dear
As all the metal in your shop will answer.
I will obey you till I give you bail.
But, peasant, this game will cost you dearly,
You'll have to pay with all the metal in your shop.

ANGELO
Sir, sir, I will have law in Ephesus,
To your notorious shame; I doubt it not.
Sir, sir, the law of Ephesus is on my side,
You will be ruined, I have no doubt.

Enter DROMIO of Syracuse, from the bay

DROMIO OF SYRACUSE
Master, there is a bark of Epidamnum
That stays but till her owner comes aboard,
And then, sir, she bears away. Our fraughtage, sir,
I have convey'd aboard; and I have bought
The oil, the balsamum and aqua-vitae.
The ship is in her trim; the merry wind
Blows fair from land: they stay for nought at all
But for their owner, master, and yourself.
Master, there is a ship from Epidamnum
That is waiting until the owner comes aboard,
And then, sir, she's going to set sail. Our luggage, sir,
I have taken aboard; and I have bought
The oil, the balm and liquor.
The ship is ready; the merry wind
Blows perfectly in our favor: they await only   Their owner, master, and yourself.
ANTIPHOLUS OF EPHESUS
How now! a madman! Why, thou peevish sheep,
What ship of Epidamnum stays for me?
What's this! a madman! Why, you stupid sheep,
What ship of Epidamnum waits for me?

DROMIO OF SYRACUSE
A ship you sent me to, to hire waftage.
A ship you sent me to, to hire passage.
ANTIPHOLUS OF EPHESUS
Thou drunken slave, I sent thee for a rope;
And told thee to what purpose and what end.
You drunken slave, I sent you for a rope;
And told you to what purpose and what end.

DROMIO OF SYRACUSE
You sent me for a rope's end as soon:
You sent me to the bay, sir, for a bark.
You sent me for a whipping as soon:
You sent me to the bay, sir, for a ship.

ANTIPHOLUS OF EPHESUS
I will debate this matter at more leisure
And teach your ears to list me with more heed.
To Adriana, villain, hie thee straight:
Give her this key, and tell her, in the desk
That's cover'd o'er with Turkish tapestry,
There is a purse of ducats; let her send it:
Tell her I am arrested in the street
And that shall bail me; hie thee, slave, be gone!
On, officer, to prison till it come.
I will debate this matter when I have time
And teach your ears to listen more carefully.
To Adriana, idiot, go straight there:
Give her this key, and tell her, in the desk
That's covered over with Turkish tapestry,
There is a purse of ducats; let her send it:
Tell her I am arrested in the street
And that will bail me; get going, slave, be gone!
Go on, officer, to prison till that money comes.

Exeunt Second Merchant, Angelo, Officer, and Antipholus of Ephesus

DROMIO OF SYRACUSE
To Adriana! that is where we dined,
Where Dowsabel did claim me for her husband:
She is too big, I hope, for me to compass.
Thither I must, although against my will,
For servants must their masters' minds fulfil.
To Adriana! that is where we dined,
Where that woman said I was her husband:
She is too big, I hope, for me to handle.
I must go there, although against my will,
Servants must do whatever their masters want.

Exit

SCENE II. The house of ANTIPHOLUS of Ephesus.

Enter ADRIANA and LUCIANA

ADRIANA
Ah, Luciana, did he tempt thee so?
Mightst thou perceive austerely in his eye
That he did plead in earnest? yea or no?
Look'd he or red or pale, or sad or merrily?
What observation madest thou in this case
Of his heart's meteors tilting in his face?
Oh, Luciana, did he really tempt you like that?
Could you tell from the look in his eye
If he was actually serious? yes or no?
Was he flushed or pale, or sad or happy?
What observation did you make of his face
That could tell what he was really feeling?

LUCIANA
First he denied you had in him no right.
First he denied you had any right to him.

ADRIANA
He meant he did me none; the more my spite.
He meant he hasn't done right by me; which is true.

LUCIANA
Then swore he that he was a stranger here.
Then he swore that he was a stranger here.

ADRIANA
And true he swore, though yet forsworn he were.
True, he is acting strange, but he's lying.

LUCIANA
Then pleaded I for you.
Then pleaded I for you.

ADRIANA
And what said he?
And what did he say?

LUCIANA
That love I begg'd for you he begg'd of me.
I begged him to love you, he begged to love me.

ADRIANA
With what persuasion did he tempt thy love?
What did he say to persuade your love?

LUCIANA
With words that in an honest suit might move.
First he did praise my beauty, then my speech.
With words that might have worked in an honest setting. He praised my beauty, then my speech.

ADRIANA
Didst speak him fair?
Did you praise him too?

LUCIANA
Have patience, I beseech.
Be patient, please.

ADRIANA
I cannot, nor I will not, hold me still;
My tongue, though not my heart, shall have his will.
He is deformed, crooked, old and sere,
Ill-faced, worse bodied, shapeless everywhere;
Vicious, ungentle, foolish, blunt, unkind;
Stigmatical in making, worse in mind.
I cannot, and I will not, be still;
My tongue will have it's way if my heart can't.
He is deformed, crooked, old and withered,
Ill-faced, worse bodied, shapeless everywhere;
Vicious, ungentle, foolish, blunt, unkind;
With a deformed body, and a worse mind.

LUCIANA
Who would be jealous then of such a one?
No evil lost is wail'd when it is gone.
Why be jealous over him then?
No one cries when rid of an evil.

ADRIANA
Ah, but I think him better than I say,
And yet would herein others' eyes were worse.
Far from her nest the lapwing cries away:
My heart prays for him, though my tongue do curse.
Oh, but I think better of him than I say,
I wish he looked worse in other women's eyes.
I'm like a little crying bird, far form my nest:
My heart prays for him, though my tongue curses him.

Enter DROMIO of Syracuse

DROMIO OF SYRACUSE
Here! go; the desk, the purse! sweet, now, make haste.
Here! go; the desk, the purse! Come on, now, Hurry!

LUCIANA
How hast thou lost thy breath?
Why are you so out of breath?

DROMIO OF SYRACUSE
By running fast.
I was running fast.

ADRIANA
Where is thy master, Dromio? is he well?
Where is your master, Dromio? is he okay?

DROMIO OF SYRACUSE
No, he's in Tartar limbo, worse than hell.
A devil in an everlasting garment hath him;
One whose hard heart is button'd up with steel;
A fiend, a fury, pitiless and rough;
A wolf, nay, worse, a fellow all in buff;
A back-friend, a shoulder-clapper, one that
countermands
The passages of alleys, creeks and narrow lands;
A hound that runs counter and yet draws dryfoot well;
One that before the judgement carries poor souls to hell.
No, he's in Tartar limbo, worse than hell.
A devil in an everlasting garment has him;
One whose hard heart is buttoned up with steel;
A fiend, a fury, pitiless and rough;
A wolf, no, worse, a man in tough leather;
A betrayer, a shoulder-grabber, one that
patrols
The passages of alleys, creeks and passages
A hound that runs opposite of their prey but can still follow their tracks;
He carries poor souls to hell before they have even been judged.

ADRIANA
Why, man, what is the matter?
Why, man, what is the matter?

DROMIO OF SYRACUSE
I do not know the matter: he is 'rested on the case.
I don't know what the matter is: but he's been arrested for it.

ADRIANA
What, is he arrested? Tell me at whose suit.
What, is he arrested? Tell me on whose charge?

DROMIO OF SYRACUSE
I know not at whose suit he is arrested well;
But he's in a suit of buff which 'rested him, that can I tell.
Will you send him, mistress, redemption, the money in his desk?
I don't know who had him arrested;
But I can tell you that the man who did it was in a leather suit.
Will you send him bail, mistress, the money in his desk?

ADRIANA
Go fetch it, sister.
Go fetch it, sister.

Exit Luciana

This I wonder at,
That he, unknown to me, should be in debt.
Tell me, was he arrested on a band?
This is so strange,
That he was in debt without my knowing.
Tell me, was he arrested for a band?

DROMIO OF SYRACUSE
Not on a band, but on a stronger thing;
A chain, a chain! Do you not hear it ring?
Not a band, but on a stronger thing;
A chain, a chain! Don't you hear it ring?

ADRIANA
What, the chain?
What, the chain?

DROMIO OF SYRACUSE
No, no, the bell: 'tis time that I were gone:
It was two ere I left him, and now the clock
strikes one.
No, no, the bell: it's time for me to go:
It was two before I left him, and now the clock
strikes one.

ADRIANA
The hours come back! that did I never hear.
The hour went backwards! I've never heard that.

DROMIO OF SYRACUSE
O, yes; if any hour meet a sergeant, a' turns back for very fear.
O, yes; if any ower meet an officer, they run from fear.

ADRIANA
As if Time were in debt! how fondly dost thou reason!
As if Time were in debt! your logic is so   funny!

DROMIO OF SYRACUSE
Time is a very bankrupt, and owes more than he's worth, to season.
Nay, he's a thief too: have you not heard men say
That Time comes stealing on by night and day?
If Time be in debt and theft, and a sergeant in the way,
Hath he not reason to turn back an hour in a day?
Time is bankrupt, and owes more than he's worth or can pay back in a season.
And, he's a thief too: haven't you heard men say
That Time comes stealing on by night and day?
If Time is in debt and a thief to boot, and there's an officer in the way,
Don't you think that's reason to turn back an hour?

Re-enter LUCIANA with a purse

ADRIANA
Go, Dromio; there's the money, bear it straight;
And bring thy master home immediately.
Come, sister: I am press'd down with conceit--
Conceit, my comfort and my injury.
Go, Dromio; there's the money, take it straight there;
And bring your master home immediately.
Come, sister: my imagination is spinning--
It's both comforting and depressing.

Exeunt

SCENE III. A public place.

Enter ANTIPHOLUS of Syracuse

ANTIPHOLUS OF SYRACUSE
There's not a man I meet but doth salute me
As if I were their well-acquainted friend;
And every one doth call me by my name.
Some tender money to me; some invite me;
Some other give me thanks for kindnesses;
Some offer me commodities to buy:
Even now a tailor call'd me in his shop
And show'd me silks that he had bought for me,
And therewithal took measure of my body.
Sure, these are but imaginary wiles
And Lapland sorcerers inhabit here.

Every single man I meet greets me
As if I were their well-acquainted friend;
And every one of them calls me by my name.
Some give me money; some invite me;
Some other give me thanks for kindnesses;
Some offer me commodities to buy:
Even now a tailor called me in his shop
And showed me silks that he had bought for me,
And started taking my measurements.
I must be seeing things
There must be sorcerers living here.

Enter DROMIO OF SYRACUSE

DROMIO OF SYRACUSE
Master, here's the gold you sent me for. What, have you got the picture of old Adam new-apparelled?

Master, here's the gold you sent me for. What, have you gotten rid of that Adam, the man who was dressed in leather?

ANTIPHOLUS OF SYRACUSE
What gold is this? what Adam dost thou mean?

What gold? what man are you talking about?

DROMIO OF SYRACUSE
Not that Adam that kept the Paradise but that Adam that keeps the prison: he that goes in the calf's skin that was killed for the Prodigal; he that came behind you, sir, like an evil angel, and bid you forsake your liberty.

Not Adam that lived with Eve in Paradise but The Adam that keeps the prison: the one that was Wearing the leather clothes; the one who came Behind you, sir, like an evil angel, and arrested you.

ANTIPHOLUS OF SYRACUSE
I understand thee not.

I don't understand what you're saying.

DROMIO OF SYRACUSE
No? why, 'tis a plain case: he that went, like a
bass-viol, in a case of leather; the man, sir,
that, when gentlemen are tired, gives them a sob
and 'rests them; he, sir, that takes pity on decayed men and gives them suits of durance; he that sets up his rest to do more exploits with his mace than a morris-pike.

*No? why, it's simple: he was like a cello
cased in leather; the man, sir, that
When gentlemen are tired, gives them "arrest"
He, sir, whotakes pity on ruined men and gives them new jail clothes; he who sets out to do more harm with his mace than a soldier with a pike.*

ANTIPHOLUS OF SYRACUSE
What, thou meanest an officer?

What, you mean an officer?

DROMIO OF SYRACUSE
*Ay, sir, the sergeant of the band, he that brings
any man to answer it that breaks his band; one*

that thinks a man always going to bed, and says, 'God give you good rest!'

thinks men are always going to bed and wants to give them "arrest."

ANTIPHOLUS OF SYRACUSE
Well, sir, there rest in your foolery. Is there any ships put forth tonight? May we be gone?

Well, sir, you can stop joking there. Are there any ships setting sail tonight? Can we leave?

DROMIO OF SYRACUSE
Why, sir, I brought you word an hour since that the
bark Expedition put forth to-night; and then were
you hindered by the sergeant, to tarry for the hoy
Delay. Here are the angels that you sent for to
deliver you.

Why, sir, I told you an hour ago that the
ship Expedition is setting sail to-night; and then you
were hindered by the sergeant, and you said to wait for the rowboat Delay. Here is the bail money
you sent me to deliver to you.

ANTIPHOLUS OF SYRACUSE
The fellow is distract, and so am I;
And here we wander in illusions:
Some blessed power deliver us from hence!

This man has gone insane, and so have I;
And we are wandering in a world of illusions:
Some blessed power get us out of here!

Enter a Courtezan

Courtezan
Well met, well met, Master Antipholus.
I see, sir, you have found the goldsmith now:
Is that the chain you promised me to-day?

Well, well, good to see you Master Antipholus.
I see, sir, you have found the goldsmith now:
Is that the chain you promised me to-day?

ANTIPHOLUS OF SYRACUSE
Satan, avoid! I charge thee, tempt me not.

Satan, be gone! Don't try to tempt me.

DROMIO OF SYRACUSE
Master, is this Mistress Satan?

Master, is this Miss Satan?

ANTIPHOLUS OF SYRACUSE
It is the devil.

It is the devil.

DROMIO OF SYRACUSE
Nay, she is worse, she is the devil's dam; and here she comes in the habit of a light wench: and thereof comes that the wenches say 'God damn me;' that's as much to say 'God make me a light wench.' It is written, they appear to men like angels of light: light is an effect of fire, and fire will burn; ergo, light wenches will burn. Come not near her.

No, she is worse, she is the devil's mother; and here she comes in the guise of an easy wench: and is the reason why wenches say 'God damn me;' which is just like saying 'God make me a light wench.' In the Bible, it says they appear to men like angels of light: light is an aspect of fire, and fire will burn; therefore easy wenches will burn you. Don't go near her.

DROMIO OF SYRACUSE
Yes, sir, the sergeant of the unit, he who makes anyone answer for breaking his law; it's like he

Your man and you are marvellous merry, sir.
Will you go with me? We'll mend our dinner here?

DROMIO OF SYRACUSE
Master, if you do, expect spoon-meat; or bespeak a long spoon.

Master, if you do, expect spoon-meat; or ask for a long spoon.

ANTIPHOLUS OF SYRACUSE
Why, Dromio?

Why, Dromio?

DROMIO OF SYRACUSE
Marry, he must have a long spoon that must eat with the devil.

Of course, he who eats with the devil must have a long spoon.

ANTIPHOLUS OF SYRACUSE
Avoid then, fiend! what tell'st thou me of supping?
Thou art, as you are all, a sorceress:
I conjure thee to leave me and be gone.

Get away, demon! what dinner are you talking about?
You, like everyone else, are a sorceress:
I conjure you to leave me and be gone.

Courtezan
Give me the ring of mine you had at dinner,
Or, for my diamond, the chain you promised,
And I'll be gone, sir, and not trouble you.

Give me the ring of mine you had at dinner,
Or, in exchange, the chain you promised me,
And I'll be gone, sir, and not trouble you.

DROMIO OF SYRACUSE
Some devils ask but the parings of one's nail,
A rush, a hair, a drop of blood, a pin,
A nut, a cherry-stone;
But she, more covetous, would have a chain.
Master, be wise: an if you give it her,
The devil will shake her chain and fright us with it.

Some devils ask only for nail-clippings,
A rush, a hair, a drop of blood, a pin,
A nut, a cherry pit;
But she, greedily, would have a chain.
Master, be wise: if you give it to her,
The devil will shake her chain and frighten us with it.

Courtezan
I pray you, sir, my ring, or else the chain:
I hope you do not mean to cheat me so.

I pray you, sir, my ring, or else the chain:
I hope you're not really going to cheat me like this.

ANTIPHOLUS OF SYRACUSE
Avaunt, thou witch! Come, Dromio, let us go.

Stay away, you witch! Come, Dromio, let's go.

DROMIO OF SYRACUSE
'Fly pride,' says the peacock: mistress, that you know.

'Don't be proud,' says the peacock: mistress, you know that.

Exeunt Antipholus of Syracuse and Dromio of Syracuse

Courtezan
You and your servant are hilarious, sir.
Will you go with me? We'll finish our dinner here?

Now, out of doubt Antipholus is mad,
Else would he never so demean himself.
A ring he hath of mine worth forty ducats,
And for the same he promised me a chain:

Both one and other he denies me now.
The reason that I gather he is mad,
Besides this present instance of his rage,
Is a mad tale he told to-day at dinner,
Of his own doors being shut against his entrance.
Belike his wife, acquainted with his fits,
On purpose shut the doors against his way.
My way is now to hie home to his house,
And tell his wife that, being lunatic,
He rush'd into my house and took perforce
My ring away. This course I fittest choose;
For forty ducats is too much to lose.

Both one and other he denies me now.
The only explanation is that he's gone crazy,
Besides this strange occurrence just now,
Is the crazy story he told today at dinner,
Of being locked out of his own house.
Sounds like his wife, knew he was in a fit,
And locked him out on purpose.
I'll go now to his house,
And tell his wife that, being crazed in a fit,
He rushed into my house and took away
My ring by force. I think this is the best course;
Since forty ducats is too much money to lose.

Exit

SCENE IV. A street.

Enter ANTIPHOLUS of Ephesus and the Officer

ANTIPHOLUS OF EPHESUS
Fear me not, man; I will not break away:
I'll give thee, ere I leave thee, so much money,
To warrant thee, as I am 'rested for.
My wife is in a wayward mood to-day,
And will not lightly trust the messenger
That I should be attach'd in Ephesus,
I tell you, 'twill sound harshly in her ears.
Don't be afraid; I will not try to escape:
I'll give you, before I leave, the bail money,
You are entitled to for my arrest.
My wife is in a bad mood today,
And will not lightly trust the messenger
That tells her I've been arrested in Ephesus,
I tell you, she won't like the sound of that.

Enter DROMIO of Ephesus with a rope's-end

Here comes my man; I think he brings the money.
How now, sir! have you that I sent you for?
Here comes my servant; I think he brings the money.
What's this! do you have what I sent you for?
DROMIO OF EPHESUS
Here's that, I warrant you, will pay them all.
I promise, this will make them all pay.
ANTIPHOLUS OF EPHESUS
But where's the money?
But where's the money?

DROMIO OF EPHESUS
Why, sir, I gave the money for the rope.
Why, sir, used it to pay for the rope.
ANTIPHOLUS OF EPHESUS
Five hundred ducats, villain, for a rope?
Five hundred ducats, stupid, for a rope?

DROMIO OF EPHESUS
I'll serve you, sir, five hundred at the rate.
I could get you five hundred ropes with that.
ANTIPHOLUS OF EPHESUS
To what end did I bid thee hie thee home?
Why did I even send you home?

DROMIO OF EPHESUS
To a rope's-end, sir; and to that end am I returned.
To buy rope, and here I am, I have returned with it.
ANTIPHOLUS OF EPHESUS
And to that end, sir, I will welcome you.
And with that rope, I will welcome you.

Beating him
Beating him
Officer
Good sir, be patient.
Good sir, be patient.

DROMIO OF EPHESUS
Nay, 'tis for me to be patient; I am in adversity.
I'm the one that needs to be patient; I'm the one suffering.

Officer
Good, now, hold thy tongue.
Listen, you, hold your tongue.

DROMIO OF EPHESUS
No, rather persuade him to hold his hands.
No, you should persuade him to hold his hands.
ANTIPHOLUS OF EPHESUS
Thou whoreson, senseless villain!
You son of a bitch, senseless idiot!

DROMIO OF EPHESUS
I would I were senseless, sir, that I might not feel
your blows.
It would be nice to be senseless, sir, then I wouldn't feel you hitting me.

ANTIPHOLUS OF EPHESUS
Thou art sensible in nothing but blows, and so is an ass.
That's all you can sense is beatings, just like an ass.

DROMIO OF EPHESUS
I am an ass, indeed; you may prove it by my long
ears. I have served him from the hour of my
nativity to this instant, and have nothing at his
hands for my service but blows. When I am cold, he heats me with beating; when I am warm, he
cools me with beating; I am waked with it when I sleep; raised with it when I sit; driven out of
doors with it when I go from home; welcomed home with it when I return; nay, I bear it on my
shoulders, as a beggar wont her brat; and, I think when he hath lamed me, I shall beg with it from
door to door.
I am an ass, indeed; you can prove it by my long
ears. I have served him from the hour of my
birth to this instant, and he has given me nothing for my service but beatings. When I am cold, he
heats me with beating; when I am warm, he cools me with beating; I woken up with it when I
sleep; raised with it when I sit; chase out of the house with it when I leave; welcomed home with it
when I return; No, I bear the bruises on my shoulders, like a beggar woman carries her brat; and,
I think once he's crippled me, I use my bruises to beg from door to door.
ANTIPHOLUS OF EPHESUS
Come, go along; my wife is coming yonder.
Alright, enough; my wife is coming.

Enter ADRIANA, LUCIANA, the Courtezan, and PINCH

DROMIO OF EPHESUS
Mistress, 'respice finem,' respect your end; or
rather, the prophecy like the parrot, 'beware the
rope's-end.'
Mistress, 'respice finem,' think on your death; or
rather, as the parrot, says 'beware the
rope's-end.'
ANTIPHOLUS OF EPHESUS
Wilt thou still talk?
Are you still talking?

Beating him
Beating him
Courtezan
How say you now? is not your husband mad?
Now what do you say? isn't your husband crazy?

ADRIANA
His incivility confirms no less.
Good Doctor Pinch, you are a conjurer;
Establish him in his true sense again,
And I will please you what you will demand.
His terrible behavior confirms it.
Good Doctor Pinch, you are a sorcerer;
Make him come to his senses,
And I will pay you whatever you ask.

LUCIANA
Alas, how fiery and how sharp he looks!
Alas, how fiery and how angry he looks!

Courtezan
Mark how he trembles in his ecstasy!
See how he's trembling from his fit!

PINCH
Give me your hand and let me feel your pulse.
Give me your hand and let me feel your pulse.
ANTIPHOLUS OF EPHESUS
There is my hand, and let it feel your ear.
There is my hand, I'll make it feel your ear.

Striking him
Striking him
PINCH
I charge thee, Satan, housed within this man,
To yield possession to my holy prayers
And to thy state of darkness hie thee straight:
I conjure thee by all the saints in heaven!
I command you, Satan, living within this man,
Obey my holy prayers and release him,
And go straight back to your state of darkness:
I command you by all the saints in heaven!
ANTIPHOLUS OF EPHESUS
Peace, doting wizard, peace! I am not mad.
Stop, silly wizard, stop! I am not crazy.

ADRIANA
O, that thou wert not, poor distressed soul!
O, I wish you weren't, poor distressed soul!

ANTIPHOLUS OF EPHESUS
You minion, you, are these your customers?
Did this companion with the saffron face
Revel and feast it at my house to-day,
Whilst upon me the guilty doors were shut
And I denied to enter in my house?
You sneak, you, are these your customers?
Did this fool with the yellow face
Revel and feast with you at my house today,
While the guilty doors were shut in my face
And denied me entrance into my own house?

ADRIANA
O husband, God doth know you dined at home;
Where would you had remain'd until this time,
Free from these slanders and this open shame!
O husband, God knows you dined at home;
Where you should have remained,
Free from these slanders and this open shame!
ANTIPHOLUS OF EPHESUS
Dined at home! Thou villain, what sayest thou?
Dined at home! You fool, what are you saying?

DROMIO OF EPHESUS
Sir, sooth to say, you did not dine at home.
I can attest, you did not dine at home.
ANTIPHOLUS OF EPHESUS
Were not my doors lock'd up and I shut out?
My doors were locked and I was shut out, right?

DROMIO OF EPHESUS
Perdie, your doors were lock'd and you shut out.
Truth, doors were locked and you were shut out.
ANTIPHOLUS OF EPHESUS
And did not she herself revile me there?
And didn't she herself yell at me?

DROMIO OF EPHESUS
Sans fable, she herself reviled you there.
No lies, she yelled at you.
ANTIPHOLUS OF EPHESUS
Did not her kitchen-maid rail, taunt, and scorn me?
Didn't her kitchen-maid yell, mock, and tease me?

DROMIO OF EPHESUS
Certes, she did; the kitchen-vestal scorn'd you.
She surely did; the kitchen-vestal mocked you.
ANTIPHOLUS OF EPHESUS
And did not I in rage depart from thence?
And I left in a rage, didn't I?

DROMIO OF EPHESUS
In verity you did; my bones bear witness,
That since have felt the vigour of his rage.
You truly did; my bones can attest
Since they've been feeling your rage.

ADRIANA
Is't good to soothe him in these contraries?
Should I soothe him by agreeing to these lies?

PINCH
It is no shame: the fellow finds his vein,
And yielding to him humours well his frenzy.
Good thinking: his servant has found out,
That the best way is to humor his insanity.
ANTIPHOLUS OF EPHESUS
Thou hast suborn'd the goldsmith to arrest me.
You the one who sent the goldsmith to arrest me.

ADRIANA
Alas, I sent you money to redeem you,
By Dromio here, who came in haste for it.
No, I sent you money to bail you out,
By Dromio here, who came in a hurry for it.

DROMIO OF EPHESUS
Money by me! heart and goodwill you might;
But surely master, not a rag of money.
Money! me! Maybe heart and goodwill;
But surely master, not a cent of money.
ANTIPHOLUS OF EPHESUS
Went'st not thou to her for a purse of ducats?
Did you not go to her for a purse of money?

ADRIANA
He came to me and I deliver'd it.
He came to me and I delivered it.

LUCIANA
And I am witness with her that she did.
And I am witness with her that she did.

DROMIO OF EPHESUS
God and the rope-maker bear me witness
That I was sent for nothing but a rope!
God and the rope-maker are my witnesses
That I was sent for nothing but a rope!

PINCH
Mistress, both man and master is possess'd;
I know it by their pale and deadly looks:
They must be bound and laid in some dark room.
Mistress, both slave and master are possessed;
I know it by their pale and deadly looks:
They need to be bound and put in a dark room.
ANTIPHOLUS OF EPHESUS
Say, wherefore didst thou lock me forth to-day?
And why dost thou deny the bag of gold?
Tell me, why did you lock me out today?
And you, why are you denying the bag of gold?

ADRIANA
I did not, gentle husband, lock thee forth.
I did not, gentle husband, lock you out.

DROMIO OF EPHESUS
And, gentle master, I received no gold;
But I confess, sir, that we were lock'd out.
And, gentle master, I received no gold;
But I confess, sir, that we were locked out.
ADRIANA
Dissembling villain, thou speak'st false in both.
Lying fool, you're lying about both.

ANTIPHOLUS OF EPHESUS
Dissembling harlot, thou art false in all;
And art confederate with a damned pack
To make a loathsome abject scorn of me:
But with these nails I'll pluck out these false eyes
That would behold in me this shameful sport.
Lying whore, everything about you is false;
And you are scheming with bad people
To make hateful, degrading fool of me:
But I'll use my nails to pluck out your lying eyes
That would see me be humiliated.

Enter three or four, and offer to bind him. He strives

ADRIANA
O, bind him, bind him! let him not come near me.
O, bind him, bind him! don't let him come near me.

PINCH
More company! The fiend is strong within him.
We need more men! The demon in him is strong.

LUCIANA
Ay me, poor man, how pale and wan he looks!
Oh my, poor man, how pale and weak he looks!
ANTIPHOLUS OF EPHESUS
What, will you murder me? Thou gaoler, thou,
I am thy prisoner: wilt thou suffer them
To make a rescue?
What, will you murder me? You jailer, you,
I am your prisoner: are you just going to let them break me out of jail?

Officer
Masters, let him go
He is my prisoner, and you shall not have him.
Masters, let him go
He is my prisoner, and you shall not have him.

PINCH
Go bind this man, for he is frantic too.
Go bind this man, for he is frantic too.

They offer to bind Dromio of Ephesus

ADRIANA
What wilt thou do, thou peevish officer?
Hast thou delight to see a wretched man
Do outrage and displeasure to himself?
What will you do, you stupid officer?
Do you take pleasure in seeing a tortured man
Upset and harm himself?

Officer
He is my prisoner: if I let him go,
The debt he owes will be required of me.
He is my prisoner: if I let him go,
I will have to pay the debt he owes.

ADRIANA
I will discharge thee ere I go from thee:
Bear me forthwith unto his creditor,
And, knowing how the debt grows, I will pay it.
Good master doctor, see him safe convey'd
Home to my house. O most unhappy day!
I'll pay you before I leave:
Take me to the person he is owing to,
And, once I know how much it is, I will pay it.
Good master doctor, see him taken safely
Home to my house. O what an awful day!
ANTIPHOLUS OF EPHESUS
O most unhappy strumpet!
O what an awful slut!

DROMIO OF EPHESUS
Master, I am here entered in bond for you.
Master, I am here tied up for you.
ANTIPHOLUS OF EPHESUS
Out on thee, villain! wherefore dost thou mad me?
Shut up already, stupid! why are you trying to provoke me?

DROMIO OF EPHESUS
Will you be bound for nothing? be mad, good master: cry 'The devil!'
Will you just be tied up for no reason? At least act insane, good master: shout 'The devil!'

LUCIANA
God help, poor souls, how idly do they talk!
God help them, poor souls, talking so strangely!

ADRIANA
Go bear him hence. Sister, go you with me.
Go take him home. Sister, go you with me.
Exeunt all but Adriana, Luciana, Officer and Courtezan

Say now, whose suit is he arrested at?
Tell me, who had him arrested?

Officer
One Angelo, a goldsmith: do you know him?
One Angelo, a goldsmith: do you know him?

ADRIANA
I know the man. What is the sum he owes?
I know the man. What is the sum he owes?

Officer
Two hundred ducats.
Two hundred ducats.

ADRIANA
Say, how grows it due?
Tell me, what is it for?

Officer
Due for a chain your husband had of him.
For a chain your husband had of him.

ADRIANA
He did bespeak a chain for me, but had it not.
He spoke of a chain for me, but I never got it.

Courtezan
When as your husband all in rage to-day
Came to my house and took away my ring--
The ring I saw upon his finger now--
Straight after did I meet him with a chain.
Then your husband came in a fit of rage
To my house and took away my ring--
The ring I saw on his finger just now--
Right after that I saw him with a chain.

ADRIANA
It may be so, but I did never see it.
Come, gaoler, bring me where the goldsmith is:
I long to know the truth hereof at large.
It may be so, but I never saw it.
Come, jailer, take me to where the goldsmith is:
I long to know the truth of all this.

Enter ANTIPHOLUS of Syracuse with his rapier drawn, and DROMIO of Syracuse

LUCIANA
God, for thy mercy! they are loose again.
God, be merciful! they are loose again.

ADRIANA
And come with naked swords.
Let's call more help to have them bound again.

And come with swords drawn.
Let's call more help to have them bound again.

Officer
Away! they'll kill us.
We need to get away! they'll kill us.

Exeunt all but Antipholus of Syracuse and Dromio of Syracuse

ANTIPHOLUS OF SYRACUSE
I see these witches are afraid of swords.
I see these witches are afraid of swords.

DROMIO OF SYRACUSE
She that would be your wife now ran from you.
The one who thinks she's your wife ran from you just now.

ANTIPHOLUS OF SYRACUSE
Come to the Centaur; fetch our stuff from thence:
I long that we were safe and sound aboard.
Come to the Centaur; let's get our things:
I can't wait until we're safe and sound aboard.

DROMIO OF SYRACUSE
Faith, stay here this night; they will surely do us
no harm: you saw they speak us fair, give us gold: methinks they are such a gentle nation that, but
for the mountain of mad flesh that claims marriage of me, I could find in my heart to stay here still
and turn witch.
I say we stay here tonight; they surely won't do
us any harm: you saw how nice they are, they give us gold: I think this would be such a gentle
place, and if it wasn't for the insane mountain of flesh that wants to marry me, I could find in my
heart to stay here and become a witch too.
ANTIPHOLUS OF SYRACUSE
I will not stay to-night for all the town;
Therefore away, to get our stuff aboard.
I won't stay another night for the whole town;
So let's go get our stuff aboard.

Exeunt

Act 5

SCENE I. A street before a Priory.

Enter Second Merchant and ANGELO

ANGELO
I am sorry, sir, that I have hinder'd you;
But, I protest, he had the chain of me,
Though most dishonestly he doth deny it.

I am sorry, sir, that I have kept you;
But, I'm telling you, he got the chain from me,
Though he is denying it so dishonestly.

Second Merchant
How is the man esteemed here in the city?

How well is the man respected here in the city?

ANGELO
Of very reverend reputation, sir,
Of credit infinite, highly beloved,
Second to none that lives here in the city:
His word might bear my wealth at any time.

He has a spotless reputation, sir,
He has unlimited credit, highly beloved,
Second to no one that lives here in the city:
I would trust him with all my money any time.

Second Merchant
Speak softly; yonder, as I think, he walks.

Speak quietly; I think he's walking over here.

Enter ANTIPHOLUS of Syracuse and DROMIO of Syracuse

ANGELO
'Tis so; and that self chain about his neck
Which he forswore most monstrously to have.
Good sir, draw near to me, I'll speak to him.
Signior Antipholus, I wonder much
That you would put me to this shame and trouble;
And, not without some scandal to yourself,
With circumstance and oaths so to deny
This chain which now you wear so openly:
Beside the charge, the shame, imprisonment,
You have done wrong to this my honest friend,
Who, but for staying on our controversy,
Had hoisted sail and put to sea to-day:
This chain you had of me; can you deny it?

It's him; and he's wearing the chain on his neck
That he swore up and down that he didn't have.
Good sir, step closer, I'll speak to him.
Mister Antipholus, I'm astonished
That you would put me through so much shame and trouble;
And, not without some scandal to yourself,
Lie and swear that you denied having
This chain which you're now wearing in public:
But money, shame, and imprisonment aside,
You have greatly wronged my honest friend,
Who, if he hadn't had to stay for this mess,
Had hoisted sail, And set out to sea today:
You did get this chain from me; can you deny it?

ANTIPHOLUS OF SYRACUSE
I think I had; I never did deny it.

Yes, I did; I never denied it.

Second Merchant
Yes, that you did, sir, and forswore it too.

Yes, you did deny it, sir, and swore it too.

ANTIPHOLUS OF SYRACUSE
Who heard me to deny it or forswear it?

Who heard me to deny it or swear it?

Second Merchant
These ears of mine, thou know'st did hear thee.
Fie on thee, wretch! 'tis pity that thou livest
To walk where any honest man resort.

ANTIPHOLUS OF SYRACUSE
Thou art a villain to impeach me thus:
I'll prove mine honour and mine honesty
Against thee presently, if thou darest stand.

You're a scoundrel to accuse me like this:
I'll defend my honor and my honesty
Against you right now, if you dare.

Second Merchant
I dare, and do defy thee for a villain.

I do dare, and I call you a scoundrel.

They draw

They draw

Enter ADRIANA, LUCIANA, the Courtezan, and others

ADRIANA
Hold, hurt him not, for God's sake! he is mad.
Some get within him, take his sword away:
Bind Dromio too, and bear them to my house.

Wait, don't hurt him, for God's sake! He's crazy.
Someone get him, take his sword away:
Bind Dromio too, and take them to my house.

DROMIO OF SYRACUSE
Run, master, run; for God's sake, take a house!
This is some priory. In, or we are spoil'd!

Run, master, run; for God's sake, hide in a house!
This is a monastery. Duck in or we're done for!

Exeunt Antipholus of Syracuse and Dromio of Syracuse to the Priory

Enter the Lady Abbess, AEMILIA

AEMELIA
Be quiet, people. Wherefore throng you hither?

Be quiet, people. What are you all doing here?

ADRIANA
To fetch my poor distracted husband hence.
Let us come in, that we may bind him fast
And bear him home for his recovery.

I'm here to get my poor insane husband back.
Let us in, so we can tie him up tight
And take him home and make him well.

ANGELO
I knew he was not in his perfect wits.

I knew something was wrong with his wits.

Second Merchant
I am sorry now that I did draw on him.

I am sorry now that I drew my sword on him.

AEMELIA
How long hath this possession held the man?

How long has he been possessed?

ADRIANA
This week he hath been heavy, sour, sad,
And much different from the man he was;
Second Merchant
These ears of mine, you know I heard you.
To hell with you, scoundrel! it's a pity you live
To walk among honest men.

This week he he's been angry, mean, sad,
And much different from the man he was;
But till this afternoon his passion
Ne'er brake into extremity of rage.

AEMELIA
Hath he not lost much wealth by wreck of sea?
Buried some dear friend? Hath not else his eye
Stray'd his affection in unlawful love?
A sin prevailing much in youthful men,
Who give their eyes the liberty of gazing.
Which of these sorrows is he subject to?

Did he lose a lot of money in a ship wreck?
Buried a dear friend? Or maybe he's been
Straying into an affair?
A sin that occurs often in young men,
Who give their eyes the freedom to gaze.
Which of these things are affecting him?

ADRIANA
To none of these, except it be the last;
Namely, some love that drew him oft from home.

None of them, except maybe the last one;
Meaning, I think there was another women that often took him from his home.

AEMELIA
You should for that have reprehended him.

You should have scolded him for that.

ADRIANA
Why, so I did.

Why, so I did.

AEMELIA
Ay, but not rough enough.

Maybe, but not rough enough.

ADRIANA
As roughly as my modesty would let me.

As roughly as my modesty would let me.

AEMELIA
Haply, in private.

Probably in private.

ADRIANA
And in assemblies too.

And in public too.

AEMELIA
Ay, but not enough.

Yes, but not enough.

ADRIANA
It was the copy of our conference:
In bed he slept not for my urging it;
At board he fed not for my urging it;
Alone, it was the subject of my theme;
In company I often glanced it;
Still did I tell him it was vile and bad.

It was the main thing we talked about:
I didn't let him sleep without bringing it up;
He couldn't eat without me bringing it up;
Alone, it was all I talked about;
When we were with others I would hint at it;
I kept telling him how evil and bad it was.

AEMELIA
And thereof came it that the man was mad.
The venom clamours of a jealous woman
Poisons more deadly than a mad dog's tooth.
It seems his sleeps were hinder'd by thy railing,
And therefore comes it that his head is light.
Thou say'st his meat was sauced with thy upbraidings:
But until this afternoon his passion
Never got so extreme that it was rage.

And that's why he went insane.
The poisonous rants of a jealous woman
Poisons more deadly than a rabid dog's bite.
It seems like he couldn't sleep with you pestering him, so his head is disoriented.
You say you seasoned his food with your scolding:
Unquiet meals make ill digestions;
Thereof the raging fire of fever bred;
And what's a fever but a fit of madness?
Thou say'st his sports were hinderd by thy

brawls:
Sweet recreation barr'd, what doth ensue
But moody and dull melancholy,
Kinsman to grim and comfortless despair,
And at her heels a huge infectious troop
Of pale distemperatures and foes to life?
In food, in sport and life-preserving rest
To be disturb'd, would mad or man or beast:
The consequence is then thy jealous fits
Have scared thy husband from the use of wits.

him:
When someone can't enjoy themselves, *They become moody and dull with melancholy,*
Close to grim and comfortless despair,
And soon after that, a whole mess
Of sicknesses and ailments
Food, fun and life-preserving rest
If disturbed, would drive any man or beast crazy:
The consequence then is that your jealous fits
Have taken away your husband from his mind.

LUCIANA
She never reprehended him but mildly,
When he demean'd himself rough, rude and wildly.
Why bear you these rebukes and answer not?

She only ever scolded him gently,
Even when he behaved himself so rough, rude and wildly.
Why aren't you defending yourself to her?

ADRIANA
She did betray me to my own reproof.
Good people enter and lay hold on him.

She has made me see my faults.
Good people, go in there and get him.

AEMELIA
No, not a creature enters in my house.

No, no one can enter in my house.

ADRIANA
Then let your servants bring my husband forth.

Then let your servants bring my husband forth.

AEMELIA
Neither: he took this place for sanctuary,
And it shall privilege him from your hands
Till I have brought him to his wits again,
Or lose my labour in assaying it.

No: he came to this place for sanctuary,
And it shall save him from your hands
Till I have brought him back to sense,
Or try to the best of my ability.

ADRIANA
I will attend my husband, be his nurse,
Diet his sickness, for it is my office,
And will have no attorney but myself;
And therefore let me have him home with me.

I will attend to my husband, be his nurse,
To heal him when he is sick, that is my job,
And will have no one do it but me;
So let me take him home with me.

AEMELIA
Be patient; for I will not let him stir
Till I have used the approved means I have,
With wholesome syrups, drugs and holy prayers,
To make of him a formal man again:
It is a branch and parcel of mine oath,
A charitable duty of my order.
Therefore depart and leave him here with me.

Be patient; I won't let him leave
Till I have done everything in my power,
With wholesome syrups, drugs and holy prayers,
To make him normal again:
Healing is a part of the religious oaths I took,
A charitable duty of my order.
So go on, and leave him here with me.

ADRIANA
I will not hence and leave my husband here:
And ill it doth beseem your holiness
To separate the husband and the wife.

I will not go and leave my husband here:

It doesn't seem very holy, your holiness,
To separate a husband from his wife.

AEMELIA
Be quiet and depart: thou shalt not have him.

Be quiet and leave: you will not have him.

Exit

LUCIANA
Complain unto the duke of this indignity.

Complain the duke of this indignity.

ADRIANA
Come, go: I will fall prostrate at his feet
And never rise until my tears and prayers
Have won his grace to come in person hither
And take perforce my husband from the abbess.

Come with me: I will fall and beg at his feet
And never rise until my tears and prayers
Have convinced his grace to come here in person
And take my husband from the nun by force.

Second Merchant
By this, I think, the dial points at five:
Anon, I'm sure, the duke himself in person
Comes this way to the melancholy vale,
The place of death and sorry execution,
Behind the ditches of the abbey here.

By this time, I think, it must be five:
Soon, I'm sure, the duke himself in person
Will come this way to the melancholy vale,
The place of death where they hold executions,
Behind the ditches of the abbey here.

ANGELO
Upon what cause?

Why is he coming?

Second Merchant
To see a reverend Syracusian merchant,
Who put unluckily into this bay
Against the laws and statutes of this town,
Beheaded publicly for his offence.

To see an elderly Syracusian merchant,
Who unluckily came ashore in this bay
Against the laws and statutes of this town,
Beheaded publicly for his offence.

ANGELO
See where they come: we will behold his death.

That's them now: we will watch his death.

LUCIANA
Kneel to the duke before he pass the abbey.

Kneel to the duke before he passes the abbey.

Enter DUKE SOLINUS, attended; AEGEON bareheaded; with the Headsman and other Officers

DUKE SOLINUS
Yet once again proclaim it publicly,
If any friend will pay the sum for him,
He shall not die; so much we tender him.

Again I publicly announce,
That if any friend will pay the sum for him,
He will not die; that's how much we like him.

ADRIANA
Justice, most sacred duke, against the abbess!

Give me justice, most sacred duke, against the nun!

DUKE SOLINUS
She is a virtuous and a reverend lady:
It cannot be that she hath done thee wrong.

She is a virtuous and a respected lady:
It can't be that she's done you wrong.

ADRIANA

May it please your grace, Antipholus, my husband,
Whom I made lord of me and all I had,
At your important letters,--this ill day
A most outrageous fit of madness took him;
That desperately he hurried through the street,
With him his bondman, all as mad as he--
Doing displeasure to the citizens
By rushing in their houses, bearing thence
Rings, jewels, any thing his rage did like.
Once did I get him bound and sent him home,
Whilst to take order for the wrongs I went,
That here and there his fury had committed.
Anon, I wot not by what strong escape,
He broke from those that had the guard of him;
And with his mad attendant and himself,
Each one with ireful passion, with drawn swords,
Met us again and madly bent on us,
Chased us away; till, raising of more aid,
We came again to bind them. Then they fled
Into this abbey, whither we pursued them:
And here the abbess shuts the gates on us
And will not suffer us to fetch him out,
Nor send him forth that we may bear him hence.
Therefore, most gracious duke, with thy command
Let him be brought forth and borne hence for help.

May it please your grace, Antipholus, my husband,
Who I married and gave all I had,
Because of your letters,--this horrible day
An outrageous fit of madness took over him;
And he ran desperately through the streets,
With his servant man, just as crazed--
Doing mean things to the citizens
By rushing in their houses, and taking away
Rings, jewels, any thing his rage wanted.
Once I finally got him tied up, I sent him home,
So that I could mend the damage he caused
All day going here and there in a fury.
Soon, I supposed by brute force he escaped,
He broke away from the men guarding him;
And with his mad attendant and himself,
Both fiery with anger, with drawn swords,
Found us again and madly bent on us killing us,
Chased us away; till, we could get more help,
We came again to tie them up. Then they fled
Into this abbey, where we pursued them:
And then the nun shuts the gates on us
And will let us in to get him out,
Or send him out to so that we can take him home.
Therefore, most gracious duke, please
Command that he be brought out and taken away to get help.

DUKE SOLINUS
Long since thy husband served me in my wars,
And I to thee engaged a prince's word,
When thou didst make him master of thy bed,
To do him all the grace and good I could.
Go, some of you, knock at the abbey-gate
And bid the lady abbess come to me.
I will determine this before I stir.

Long ago, your husband served my in my wars,
And I promised you, a prince's word,
That when you made him master of your bed,
That I would do all I could for him.
Go, some of you, knock at the abbey-gate
And ask the lady nun to come to me.
I will settle this before we continue on.

Enter a Servant

Servant
O mistress, mistress, shift and save yourself!
My master and his man are both broke loose,
Beaten the maids a-row and bound the doctor
Whose beard they have singed off with brands of fire;
And ever, as it blazed, they threw on him
Great pails of puddled mire to quench the hair:
My master preaches patience to him and the while
Servant
O mistress, mistress, go and save yourself!
My master and his man have both broken loose,
They beat all the maids, and tied up the doctor
Whose beard they have singed off with firery brands;
And as it burned and blazed they threw
Huge pails of sweage to put it out:
My master tells him to be patient and calm, and while he does that

His man with scissors nicks him like a fool,
And sure, unless you send some present help,
Between them they will kill the conjurer.

His servant cuts his hair to make him look a fool,
I'm certain, unless you send some help soon,
Between them they will kill the sorcerer.

ADRIANA
Peace, fool! thy master and his man are here,
And that is false thou dost report to us.

Quiet, fool! your master and his servant are here,
And everything you're reporting to us is a lie.

Servant
Mistress, upon my life, I tell you true;
I have not breathed almost since I did see it.
He cries for you, and vows, if he can take you,
To scorch your face and to disfigure you.

Mistress, I swear on my life, I tell the truth;
I almost haven't breathed since I saw it.
He screams for you, and swears, if he finds you
He'll scorch your face and disfigure you.

Cry within

Cry within

Hark, hark! I hear him, mistress. fly, be gone!

There, there! I hear him, mistress. Run, go on!

DUKE SOLINUS
Come, stand by me; fear nothing. Guard with halberds!

Come, stand by me; don't be afraid. Guards bring your weapons!

ADRIANA
Ay me, it is my husband! Witness you,
That he is borne about invisible:
Even now we housed him in the abbey here;
And now he's there, past thought of human reason.

Oh my, it is my husband! Look everyone,
He walks around, invisible:
Just now we saw him in the abbey here;
And now he's there, it's impossible to understand.

Enter ANTIPHOLUS of Ephesus and DROMIO of Ephesus

ANTIPHOLUS OF EPHESUS
Justice, most gracious duke, O, grant me justice!
Even for the service that long since I did thee,
When I bestrid thee in the wars and took
Deep scars to save thy life; even for the blood
That then I lost for thee, now grant me justice.

Justice, most gracious duke, O, grant me justice!
For the service I did for you , long ago,
When I stood by you in the wars, and took
Deep scars to save your life; even for the blood
That I lost then for you, now grant me justice.

AEGEON
Unless the fear of death doth make me dote,
I see my son Antipholus and Dromio.

Unless the fear of death is making me see things,
I see my son Antipholus and Dromio.

ANTIPHOLUS OF EPHESUS
Justice, sweet prince, against that woman there!
She whom thou gavest to me to be my wife,
That hath abused and dishonour'd me
Even in the strength and height of injury!
Beyond imagination is the wrong
That she this day hath shameless thrown on me.

Justice, sweet prince, against that woman there!
She whom you have to me to be my wife,
Who has abused and dishonored me
Adding insult to injury!
The wrongdoing is beyond imagining
That she has shamelessly done to me today.

DUKE SOLINUS
Discover how, and thou shalt find me just.

Tell me how, and I will be fair.

ANTIPHOLUS OF EPHESUS
This day, great duke, she shut the doors upon me,
While she with harlots feasted in my house.

This day, great duke, she locked me out of my own doors,
While she feasted with whores in my house.

DUKE SOLINUS
A grievous fault! Say, woman, didst thou so?

How horrible! Tell me, woman, did you do that?

ADRIANA
No, my good lord: myself, he and my sister
To-day did dine together. So befall my soul
As this is false he burdens me withal!

No, my good lord: myself, he and my sister
Dined together today. May my soul be damned
If what he said was true!

LUCIANA
Ne'er may I look on day, nor sleep on night,
But she tells to your highness simple truth!

May I never see another day, or sleep at night,
If she isn't telling the truth!

ANGELO
O perjured woman! They are both forsworn:
In this the madman justly chargeth them.

O damnable woman! They are both lying:
The madmen is telling the truth about that.

ANTIPHOLUS OF EPHESUS
My liege, I am advised what I say,
Neither disturbed with the effect of wine,
Nor heady-rash, provoked with raging ire,
Albeit my wrongs might make one wiser mad.
This woman lock'd me out this day from dinner:
That goldsmith there, were he not pack'd with her,
Could witness it, for he was with me then;
Who parted with me to go fetch a chain,
Promising to bring it to the Porpentine,
Where Balthazar and I did dine together.
Our dinner done, and he not coming thither,
I went to seek him: in the street I met him
And in his company that gentleman.
There did this perjured goldsmith swear me down
That I this day of him received the chain,
Which, God he knows, I saw not: for the which
He did arrest me with an officer.
I did obey, and sent my peasant home
For certain ducats: he with none return'd
Then fairly I bespoke the officer
To go in person with me to my house.
By the way we met
My wife, her sister, and a rabble more
Of vile confederates. Along with them
My liege, I know what I am saying,
I am not confused with the effect of wine,
Or headstrong, provoked by rage and anger,
Though the wrongs I've suffered might drive a wiser man insane.
This woman locked me out today for dinner:
That goldsmith there, if he weren't on her side,
Could witness it, since he was with me then;
He left to go fetch a chain,
And promised bring it to the Porpentine,
Where Balthazar and I dined together.
Once we were done, since he never came,
I went to seek him: I met him in the street
And he was in the company of that gentleman.
Then that damned goldsmith swore up and down,
That earlier in the day he gave me the chain,
Which, God knows, I never saw: then   *He had an officer arrest me.*
I obeyed, and sent my servant home
For bail money: he came back without it
So I told the officer

To go in person with me to my house.
On the way we met
My wife, her sister, and a huge group
Of her awful companions. Along with them

They brought one Pinch, a hungry lean-faced villain,
A mere anatomy, a mountebank,
A threadbare juggler and a fortune-teller,
A needy, hollow-eyed, sharp-looking wretch,
A dead-looking man: this pernicious slave,
Forsooth, took on him as a conjurer,
And, gazing in mine eyes, feeling my pulse,
And with no face, as 'twere, outfacing me,
Cries out, I was possess'd. Then all together
They fell upon me, bound me, bore me thence
And in a dark and dankish vault at home
There left me and my man, both bound together;
Till, gnawing with my teeth my bonds in sunder,
I gain'd my freedom, and immediately
Ran hither to your grace; whom I beseech
To give me ample satisfaction
For these deep shames and great indignities.

They brought a Pinch, a hungry lean-faced villain,   *A*
skeleton, a quack, impostor,
A raggedy magician and a fortune-teller,
A needy, hollow-eyed, sharp-looking wretch,
A dead-looking man: this noxious slave,
Pretended like he was a sorcerer,
And, gazing into my eyes, feeling my pulse,
And with this thin face facing me,
Cried out, that I was possessed. Then all together
They came at me, bound me, and took me away
And in a dark, dank vault in my home
They left me and my servant, tied together;
Till I gnawed through the ropes,
And I gained my freedom, and immediately
Ran this way to you; whom I implore
To give me my due satisfaction
For these deep shames and great indignities.

ANGELO
My lord, in truth, thus far I witness with him,
That he dined not at home, but was lock'd out.

My lord, truthfully, I can vouch for him on this,
He did not dine at home since he was locked out.

DUKE SOLINUS
But had he such a chain of thee or no?

But did he get that chain from you or no?

ANGELO
He had, my lord: and when he ran in here,
These people saw the chain about his neck.

He did, my lord: and when he ran in just now,
These people saw the chain about his neck.

Second Merchant
Besides, I will be sworn these ears of mine
Heard you confess you had the chain of him
After you first forswore it on the mart:
And thereupon I drew my sword on you;
And then you fled into this abbey here,
From whence, I think, you are come by miracle.

Besides, I swear these ears of mine
Heard you confess you got the chain from him
After you swore at the mart that you didn't:
And that's when I drew my sword on you;
And then you fled into this abbey here,
And by some miracle have come out.

ANTIPHOLUS OF EPHESUS
I never came within these abbey-walls,
Nor ever didst thou draw thy sword on me:
I never saw the chain, so help me Heaven!
And this is false you burden me withal.

I never came within these abbey-walls,
And you have never drawn your sword on me:
I never saw the chain, so help me Heaven!
All these things you say about me are lies.

DUKE SOLINUS
Why, what an intricate impeach is this!
I think you all have drunk of Circe's cup.
If here you housed him, here he would have been;
If he were mad, he would not plead so coldly:
You say he dined at home; the goldsmith here
Denies that saying. Sirrah, what say you?

Why, what an intricate case this is!
I think you have all drunk of Circe's cup and been turned into animals.
If you kept him here, he would still be here;
If he were insane, he would not talk so calmly:
You say he dined at home; the goldsmith here
Denies that. Slave, what do you say?

DROMIO OF EPHESUS
Sir, he dined with her there, at the Porpentine.

Sir, he dined with that lady, at the Porpentine.

Courtezan
He did, and from my finger snatch'd that ring.

He did, and snatched that ring off my finger.

ANTIPHOLUS OF EPHESUS
'Tis true, my liege; this ring I had of her.

That's true, my liege; I got this ring from her.

DUKE SOLINUS
Saw'st thou him enter at the abbey here?

Did you see him enter the abbey here?

Courtezan
As sure, my liege, as I do see your grace.

As sure, my liege, as I see you now.

DUKE SOLINUS
Why, this is strange. Go call the abbess hither.
I think you are all mated or stark mad.

Why, this is strange. Go call the nun out here.
I think you are all confused or totally insane.

Exit one to Abbess

AEGEON
Most mighty duke, vouchsafe me speak a word:
Haply I see a friend will save my life
And pay the sum that may deliver me.

Most mighty duke, please let me speak a word:
It may be that I see a friend that will save my life
And pay the sum that will free me.

DUKE SOLINUS
Speak freely, Syracusian, what thou wilt.

Speak freely, Syracusian, say what you will.

AEGEON
Is not your name, sir, call'd Antipholus?
And is not that your bondman, Dromio?

Isn't your name, sir, called Antipholus?
And isn't that your bondman, Dromio?

DROMIO OF EPHESUS
Within this hour I was his bondman sir,
But he, I thank him, gnaw'd in two my cords:
Now am I Dromio and his man unbound.

A little while ago I was his bond man,
But thankfully he chewed through my bonds:
Now am I Dromiom his man, unbound.

AEGEON
I am sure you both of you remember me.

I am sure you both of you remember me.

DROMIO OF EPHESUS
Ourselves we do remember, sir, by you;
For lately we were bound, as you are now
You are not Pinch's patient, are you, sir?

You remind us of ourselves, sir;
Since we were just tied up like you are now
You are not Pinch's patient, are you, sir?

AEGEON
Why look you strange on me? you know me well.

Why do you look at me like a stranger? you know me well.

ANTIPHOLUS OF EPHESUS
I never saw you in my life till now.

I never saw you in my life till now.

AEGEON
O, grief hath changed me since you saw me last,
And careful hours with time's deformed hand
Have written strange defeatures in my face:
But tell me yet, dost thou not know my voice?

O, grief has changed me since you saw me last,
And time's deformed hand carefully over the hours has written strange disfigurements in my face:
But tell me, don't you know my voice?

ANTIPHOLUS OF EPHESUS
Neither.

No, not that either.

AEGEON
Dromio, nor thou?

Dromio, you don't?

DROMIO OF EPHESUS
No, trust me, sir, nor I.

No, trust me, sir, I don't.

AEGEON
I am sure thou dost.

I am sure you do.

DROMIO OF EPHESUS
Ay, sir, but I am sure I do not; and whatsoever a
man denies, you are now bound to believe him.

Yes, sir, but I am sure I do not; and since you are all bound up, you have to believe my denial.

AEGEON
Not know my voice! O time's extremity,
Hast thou so crack'd and splitted my poor tongue
In seven short years, that here my only son
Knows not my feeble key of untuned cares?
Though now this grained face of mine be hid
In sap-consuming winter's drizzled snow,
And all the conduits of my blood froze up,
Yet hath my night of life some memory,
My wasting lamps some fading glimmer left,
My dull deaf ears a little use to hear:
All these old witnesses--I cannot err--
Tell me thou art my son Antipholus.

They don't know my voice! O time's severity,
Have you cracked and splitted my poor tongue
So much that in seven years that my only son
Can't remember my weak and worried voice?
Even though my wrinkled face is hidden
In a white beard in my life's winter,
And all the veins of my blood have frozen up,
Yet at the end of my life I have some memory,
My fading eyes still have a glimmer in them,
My dull deaf ears a can still hear a little:
All my aging senses tell me--I can't be wrong--
Tell me you are my son Antipholus.

ANTIPHOLUS OF EPHESUS
I never saw my father in my life.

I've never seen my father in my life.

AEGEON
But seven years since, in Syracusa, boy,
Thou know'st we parted: but perhaps, my son,
Thou shamest to acknowledge me in misery.

But seven years ago, in Syracusa, boy,
You know we parted: but perhaps, my son,
You're ashamed acknowledge me as a prisoner.

ANTIPHOLUS OF EPHESUS
The duke and all that know me in the city
Can witness with me that it is not so
I ne'er saw Syracusa in my life.

The duke and all that know me in the city
Can tell that this is not true
I've never been to Syracusa in my life.

DUKE SOLINUS
I tell thee, Syracusian, twenty years

I tell you, Syracusian, twenty years

Have I been patron to Antipholus,
During which time he ne'er saw Syracusa:
I see thy age and dangers make thee dote.

I've been patron to Antipholus,
During which time he never saw Syracusa:
Your age and sentence have you seeing things.

Re-enter AEMILIA, with ANTIPHOLUS of Syracuse and DROMIO of Syracuse

AEMELIA
Most mighty duke, behold a man much wrong'd.

Most mighty duke, here is a man much wronged.

All gather to see them

All gather to see them

ADRIANA
I see two husbands, or mine eyes deceive me.

I see two husbands, or my eyes deceive me.

DUKE SOLINUS
One of these men is Genius to the other;
And so of these. Which is the natural man,
And which the spirit? who deciphers them?

One of these men is Spirit to the other;
And the same with these. Which is the man, and which the spirit? who can tell them apart?

DROMIO OF SYRACUSE
I, sir, am Dromio; command him away.

I, sir, am Dromio; command him away.

DROMIO OF EPHESUS
I, sir, am Dromio; pray, let me stay.

I, sir, am Dromio; please, let me stay.

ANTIPHOLUS OF SYRACUSE
Aegeon art thou not? or else his ghost?

Can it be Aegeon? or else his ghost?

DROMIO OF SYRACUSE
O, my old master! who hath bound him here?

O, my old master! Who has tied him up?

AEMELIA
Whoever bound him, I will loose his bonds
And gain a husband by his liberty.
Speak, old Aegeon, if thou be'st the man
That hadst a wife once call'd Aemilia
That bore thee at a burden two fair sons:
O, if thou be'st the same Aegeon, speak,
And speak unto the same Aemilia!

Whoever bound him, I will loose his bonds
And gain a husband by his release.
Speak, old Aegeon, if you are the man
That once had a wife called Aemilia
That bore you two sons:
O, if you are the same Aegeon, speak,
And speak here to the same Aemilia!

AEGEON
If I dream not, thou art AEmilia:
If thou art she, tell me where is that son
That floated with thee on the fatal raft?

If I'm not dreaming, you are Aemilia:
If you are her, tell me where is that son
That floated with you on the deadly raft?

AEMELIA
By men of Epidamnum he and I
And the twin Dromio all were taken up;
But by and by rude fishermen of Corinth
By force took Dromio and my son from them
And me they left with those of Epidamnum.
By men from Epidamnum he and I
And the twin Dromio all were taken up;
But later on bad fishermen from Corinth
Took Dromio and my son from them by force
And me they left with the Epidamnum men.

What then became of them I cannot tell
I to this fortune that you see me in.

I never knew what became of them
You see what happened with me.

DUKE SOLINUS
Why, here begins his morning story right;
These two Antipholuses, these two so like,
And these two Dromios, one in semblance,--
Besides her urging of her wreck at sea,--
These are the parents to these children,
Which accidentally are met together.
Antipholus, thou camest from Corinth first?

Why, here continues the story from this morning;
These two Antipholuses, these two so alike,
And these two Dromios, perfect replicas,--
Her story of being wrecked at sea,--
These are the parents to these children,
Which have met together accidentally.
Antipholus, did you come from Corinth first?

ANTIPHOLUS OF SYRACUSE
No, sir, not I; I came from Syracuse.

No, sir, not me; I came from Syracuse.

DUKE SOLINUS
Stay, stand apart; I know not which is which.

Wait, stand apart; I can't tell who is who.

ANTIPHOLUS OF EPHESUS
I came from Corinth, my most gracious lord,--

I came from Corinth, my most gracious lord,--

DROMIO OF EPHESUS
And I with him.

And I with him.

ANTIPHOLUS OF EPHESUS
Brought to this town by that most famous warrior,
Duke Menaphon, your most renowned uncle.

I was brought to this town by that most famous warrior,
Duke Menaphon, your most renowned uncle.

ADRIANA
Which of you two did dine with me to-day?

Which of you two dined with me today?

ANTIPHOLUS OF SYRACUSE
I, gentle mistress.

I, gentle mistress.

ADRIANA
And are not you my husband?

And are not you my husband?

ANTIPHOLUS OF EPHESUS
No; I say nay to that.

No; I say he's definitely not.

ANTIPHOLUS OF SYRACUSE
And so do I; yet did she call me so:
And this fair gentlewoman, her sister here,
Did call me brother.

And so do I; but she did call me that:
And this beautiful lady, her sister here,
Called me brother.

To Luciana

To Luciana

What I told you then,
I hope I shall have leisure to make good;
If this be not a dream I see and hear.

What I told you then,
I hope I can have the honor of making good on it; if all that I see and hear turns out to be real.

ANGELO
That is the chain, sir, which you had of me.

That is the chain, sir, which you had of me.

ANTIPHOLUS OF SYRACUSE
I think it be, sir; I deny it not.

I think it is, sir; I don't deny it.

ANTIPHOLUS OF EPHESUS
And you, sir, for this chain arrested me.

And you, sir, arrested me for this chain.

ANGELO
I think I did, sir; I deny it not.

I think I did, sir; I don't deny it.

ADRIANA
I sent you money, sir, to be your bail,
By Dromio; but I think he brought it not.

I sent you money, sir, to be your bail,
By Dromio; but I don't think he ever brought it.

DROMIO OF EPHESUS
No, none by me.

No, not by me

ANTIPHOLUS OF SYRACUSE
This purse of ducats I received from you,
And Dromio, my man, did bring them me.
I see we still did meet each other's man,
And I was ta'en for him, and he for me,
And thereupon these errors are arose.

This purse of ducats I received from you,
And Dromio, my servant, brought them to me.
I see met each other's servants,
And I was taken for him, and he for me,
And that's how all these errors happened.

ANTIPHOLUS OF EPHESUS
These ducats pawn I for my father here.

These ducats I use to pay for my father here.

DUKE SOLINUS
It shall not need; thy father hath his life.

There's no need; I give your father his life.

Courtezan
Sir, I must have that diamond from you.

Sir, I must have that diamond from you.

ANTIPHOLUS OF EPHESUS
There, take it; and much thanks for my good cheer.

There, take it; and much thanks for putting me in such a good mood.

AEMELIA
Renowned duke, vouchsafe to take the pains
Renowned duke, if you would take the trouble

To go with us into the abbey here
And hear at large discoursed all our fortunes:
And all that are assembled in this place,
That by this sympathized one day's error
Have suffer'd wrong, go keep us company,
And we shall make full satisfaction.
Thirty-three years have I but gone in travail
Of you, my sons; and till this present hour
My heavy burden ne'er delivered.
The duke, my husband and my children both,
And you the calendars of their nativity,
Go to a gossips' feast and go with me;
After so long grief, such festivity!

To go with us into the abbey here
And discuss at length our stories:
And anyone else assembles here,
Who in one day of confusion and error
Have suffered a wrong, come with us,
And we shall make sure everything is settled.
Thirty-three years have I been in labor
Waiting to hear of you, my sons; and have only just now been delivered of my burden.
The duke, my husband and my children both,
And you the twins of the same birth date,
Come let me christen you again in the abbey;
After so much grief, we will celebrate!

DUKE SOLINUS
With all my heart, I'll gossip at this feast.

With all my heart, I'll join this feast.

Exeunt all but Antipholus of Syracuse, Antipholus of Ephesus, Dromio of Syracuse and Dromio of Ephesus

DROMIO OF SYRACUSE
Master, shall I fetch your stuff from shipboard?

Master, shall I fetch your stuff from the ship?

ANTIPHOLUS OF EPHESUS
Dromio, what stuff of mine hast thou embark'd?

Dromio, what stuff of mine have you embarked?

DROMIO OF SYRACUSE
Your goods that lay at host, sir, in the Centaur.

Your belongings that were at the Centaur, sir.

ANTIPHOLUS OF SYRACUSE
He speaks to me. I am your master, Dromio:
Come, go with us; we'll look to that anon:
Embrace thy brother there; rejoice with him.

He means me. I am your master, Dromio:
Come with us; we'll take care of that later:
Embrace your brother there; rejoice with him.

Exeunt Antipholus of Syracuse and Antipholus of Ephesus

DROMIO OF SYRACUSE
There is a fat friend at your master's house,
That kitchen'd me for you to-day at dinner:
She now shall be my sister, not my wife.

There is a fat friend at your master's house,
That took me for you today at dinner:
Looks like she'll be my sister, not my wife.

DROMIO OF EPHESUS
Methinks you are my glass, and not my brother:
I see by you I am a sweet-faced youth.
Will you walk in to see their gossiping?

I think you're a mirror, and not my brother:
I see by you I'm a good-looking guy.
Will go with me to see their gossiping?

DROMIO OF SYRACUSE
Not I, sir; you are my elder.

No, you first, sir; you are my elder.

DROMIO OF EPHESUS
That's a question: how shall we try it?

Good question: how do we know who's older?

DROMIO OF SYRACUSE
We'll draw cuts for the senior: till then lead thou first.

We'll draw straws for who's older: till then you go first.

DROMIO OF EPHESUS
Nay, then, thus:
We came into the world like brother and brother;
And now let's go hand in hand, not one before another.

No, you know what, let's do this:
We came into the world like brother and brother;
And now let's go hand in hand, not one before another.

Exeunt

22415641R00070

Made in the USA
Lexington, KY
26 April 2013